The Desperation Game

and other stories from the
Scottish Arts Trust Story Awards

(Volume 1: 2014-2018)

Edited by Sara Cameron McBean
and Hilary Munro

Scottish Arts Trust

Scottish Arts Trust
Scottish Arts Club Charitable Trust
Scottish Charity number SC044753

Cover: *Passing Fancies* by Gordon Mitchell

IBSN: 978-1-095-632888

Scottish Arts Trust
Registered Office
SACCT
24 Rutland Square
Edinburgh
EH1 2BW
United Kingdom

Acknowledgements

Alexander McCall Smith has been the chief judge of the Scottish Arts Club Short Story Competition from its inception. We are grateful for his encouragement and support. Our thanks also to award-winning writer Sandra Ireland who took on the role of chief judge in the Edinburgh International Flash Fiction Awards. Sandra also lends the title of her prize-winning story to this anthology. Isobel Lodge was a much-loved member of the Scottish Arts Club Writers Group. We are grateful to her husband John for the donation that enabled us to keep her memory alive with the award offered in her name, and for the encouragement this gives to countless unpublished writers born, living or studying in Scotland.

Many members of the Scottish Arts Club and several others outside the club, have given their time, energy and passion to reading and re-reading the stories entered in our competitions. Their passion for discussing, debating and making the case for the stories they love is a sheer delight. We are also indebted to Dai Lowe who works tirelessly as our story awards administrator and to Michael Hamish Glen for proof-reading the publication.

A huge thank you to the Scottish Arts Trust and the Council of the Scottish Arts Club, who have collaborated on the story awards from the beginning. We look forward to many more of those sumptuous and always sold-out Story Award Dinners.

Finally, a huge thank you to all the writers who have imagined, drafted, written, re-written and submitted stories over the years. Your stories are the stuff of dreams, of inspiration and a towering, irresistible creative spirit.

"There is no greater agony than
bearing an untold story inside you."

Maya Angelou
I know why the caged bird sings

Contents

The Desperation Game
by Sandra Ireland

Winner, Scottish Arts Club Short Story Competition 2014

I paused when I got to the corner. I wanted to regroup, to ask myself again whether I really wanted to go through with this. Stooping awkwardly, I ran a finger around the back of my shoe, easing it away from the blister which was already forming. My soles were burning. That's what you get, I told myself, for slopping around in trainers. My flesh had simply forgotten how to be smart, how to market itself in black velvet and high heels.

I rummaged through my handbag for the cigarettes I knew were in there. I hadn't had a smoke since the last time I'd used this bag. It was my dating handbag and held all the essentials for a first date; mobile phone, perfume, lipstick, breath mints, a diary to note down the time and place of the second date, cigarettes for stress, tissues for tears and pepper spray if things turned ugly. They usually did. At one point my life had become one long round of first dates and I'd been so disillusioned, so stressed, I'd had to take a long hiatus from the whole scene. I'd been contemplating a life of cat-whispering and ready meals for one, until I'd heard about Deborah.

I pursed my glossy lips around a cigarette, lit it and inhaled with satisfaction. I'd first encountered Deborah's name on a business card, pushed towards me discreetly across a Formica table. My friend Carol urged me to take it.

"She doesn't advertise," Carol had whispered from behind a foaming cappuccino. "And she doesn't take on *anyone*. She's very choosy."

"So, what makes you think she'd choose me?" I picked up the card and peered at it. Deborah's name glinted like silver thread in the glare of the café's fluorescent lights. The card was ivory, expensive, confident.

"What have you got to lose?" Carol shrugged. "Remember June Harrison?"

"The one with Eighties perm and the laugh like a donkey braying?"

"Yes. Well she's just got engaged to a top heart consultant."

"No! How did she meet him?"

"*Deborah.*" Carol grinned smugly and sipped her coffee. "She's the business. Give her a call. You won't regret it."

I called her as soon as I got home. Deborah's voice was husky on the phone, very Home Counties; the kind of voice you hear advertising good coffee or expensive liqueurs. She was just as classy in the flesh when I met her three days later. Her home was a flat over a china shop, accessed by an outside staircase with iron railings. It was freshly painted, with pots of geraniums everywhere and Deborah met me at the door. She was older than I thought she'd be, but with good skin and dark hair tied back with a flowery scarf. She must like flowers, I thought. She was dressed in a rose-print tea dress and the place smelled heavily of lilies. She showed me into a sitting room with forest green walls, left me to get comfy in a leather armchair and returned moments later with a laden tray. The fire was on. A clock marked out the minutes on a pine mantle-piece and she handed me a steaming teacup and a chocolate digestive. It was all so civilised, so polite. I would have bought whatever she was selling.

Selling is entirely the wrong word. Far too common. Deborah agreed a fair price for her services, and in exchange she promised to provide me with a perfect match. Producing a leather-bound notebook and a silver pencil, she began to fire questions at me. These were interspersed with nuggets of advice. It became obvious that Deborah was an expert on the trials of the older woman in the dating game.

"The mistake you all make," she said pointedly, "is that you don't swoop in quickly enough."

"Swoop?" The word made me think of hideous black crows lined up on the telephone wire, waiting.

"Do you see men hanging around, waiting for better days? No, you do not. Men move on very quickly and so must you." Her eyes narrowed as she glared at me. I got a sense of the steeliness behind her head-girl likeability. "I have had a remarkable success rate with my system and there is no reason to think that it shouldn't work for you. Some may think it's a little…unorthodox, but …" She shrugged. "It depends how desperate you are." She fixed me with her eyes again and I knew it was a question. I nodded sadly.

The door of the newsagents' banged, bringing me back to the present. Two teenagers slouched past me. I could hear the dull beat of their iPods, the chink of bottles in carrier bags. I tossed my cigarette onto the pavement, ground it out with my shoe and gave myself a mental shake. Deborah had explained her system in detail. At first, I had been shocked, even argued with her, but that word *desperate* floated between us and in the end, I agreed to everything. I was to meet a gentleman called John. It wouldn't be a date, as such, more of a discreet introduction, stage-managed by Deborah's associate, Alastair. If things went okay, well, the ball was in my court.

I started to walk, crossed the road at the zebra crossing and continued along the high street. The arranged venue was just ahead, I could see cars parked and people milling about. Alastair would meet me at the door. Nervously, I straightened my jacket. It was black, as suggested by Deborah, with a silk scarf in rose pink to add a splash of colour. Alastair was easy to pick out. He was very tall, with silver hair and a smooth tan, dressed in an immaculate suit. I went right up to him and whispered my name. He smiled broadly, his eyes crinkling at the corners. I wondered if he was married. He offered me his arm and I took it.

"Let's get you seated," he said. "I'll get you a good vantage point, so you can see John and then, if you don't like what you see, you can always leave. No harm done."

His voice was so low I struggled to hear him.

"Won't that seem very rude?" I whispered back. "I mean, it's not the sort of place you can just walk out of …"

3

"A coughing fit always works," he said, so quickly I could see he was well practised. He opened the heavy oak door and ushered me inside. I smelled lilies and immediately thought of Deborah. He showed me to a seat and passed a slip of paper over.

"There's your crib sheet. I suggest you study it before you meet him…afterwards. Any questions? I have to go now."

"Erm, just one … what was her name?"

"Annie," he whispered. "It's all on the sheet. I'll introduce you to John later."

Alastair was as good as his word. It was his job, as an undertaker, to mastermind the whole affair, so it was a simple matter for him to introduce me discreetly to John when we arrived at the hotel for the ham sandwiches. John was a nice-looking man, just my type really. Obviously, given the circumstances, he wasn't at his best, but I could make allowances for that. I sent a silent thank you to Deborah as I shook John's hand.

"I'm Susan," I said. "I went to school with Annie. I'm so sorry for your loss …"

Aaron
by Michael Hamish Glen

Scottish Arts Club Short Story Finalist 2014,
Scottish Arts Club Member's Award Winner 2014

Wuppen yer een, he said; *open your eyes, laddie. Aye, an preen back yer lugs forby*. His words were an injunction; his countenance an invitation. My grandfather's voice was the unflinching Lowlander; his eyes the prudent Gael. Sixty, he was still a gangly foal: limbs, body, neck, head assembled at random with little chance of working in harness. *Wee Cuddie*, this man was called.

By Angle oot o Celt, he joshed. His father, going north to seek nirvana had met his mother coming south to find work. The labourer and the dreamer in role reversal. *Nae wonder they spawned me*, he would muse. They had set up home in Stirling because they wanted to live by the sea. *An they cried me glaikit!*

Wee Cuddie succeeded where his parents had failed. In his ramble of a crofthouse, he dared the sea to come over the in-bye wall. Rooms happened capriciously. He slept in a dunny off the kitchen, ate in the old byre, entertained wherever two chairs met.

If he'd owned an Irish setter, it would have surprised no one. It didn't when he found one, abandoned, on the shore. Matted, exhausted, shivering and eternally grateful. Dogsbody and mansbody were Darwinesque cousins, they shared a laboratory of genes. With all his subtlety assembled, he named it *Reid Erse*. I had to explain to my mother, Mrs Mortified of Morningside, why it wasn't 'coorse'.

In childhood, it was a summer treat to visit Grampa. In growing teens, it was ritual of delight to spend holidays at Wee Cuddie's. Eye-opening. Ear-bending. Mind-forming.

Whaur are they mussel-pickers? On the sand. *Aye, Ah ken, whit bit o sand?* That bit, the wet bit. *Aye, why's it wet?* 'Cos the sea's been on it. *Aye, Ah ken, bit whit is the sea daein?* Going out. *Aye, and whit are the mussel-pickers daein?* Poking in the sand. *Aye, Ah ken, why noo?* 'Cos the tide's gone out? *Aye, whit dis that mean?* Um. *Whit are the birds powkin for?* Food? *Aye, whit sort?* Mussels? *Worms, laddie, worms.*

And so, I learned about lugworms – and tides, watched as he dug carefully below the intricate soft brown coils which told tales, dropped the first worm he put in my hand, went back to the house and read the book. Wee Cuddie was a book-man.

He was also a bin-man, driving the truck – *it's cried a freighter here* – six days a week, with a book in his pocket, reading a sentence when he stopped, spilling out of the cab to help when bins, bags, boxes were piled high, arms flailing as he fed the crusher. The *Dervish* they called him. Or the *Professor*. Or just *Wee Cuddie*. They saved books for him that they found in bins.

He showed me his book on seaweed. Well, one of them. *Awa an rax me fower kins o weed.* I found five, and beamed. *Lat daub whit they are.* I named two, and sulked.

Harsh toned, soft hearted, short sentenced, long winded, he taught me the tricks of recognition. *Ken whit'll be different and leuk fur whit's different.*

Through hailstorm, sandstorm, rainstorm, snowstorm, showers, sunshine and moonshine, I paired off mergansers and eiders, separated ravens, rooks, crows and 'yehudis' – *Menuhin's craws* he said – grateful there were no jackdaws – or were there? *Wuppen yer een* rang in my ears.

Eyes closed, I could tell a curlew's voice at a furlong, in anger and in sorrow. The fretful beep of *mussel-pickers* was soon unlike the restless chee-rupp of *scoot-aboots*, Grampa's ringed plovers. Proudly, I announced the redshank's return, its pi-li-li-liu the progenitor, they say, of Gaelic lament. *Preen back yer lugs* guided my eyes.

Ye'll ken mair nor me, yin day. From a Scot, even a Gael-Scot, this was acclaim. I smothered a simper. <u>Yin</u> *day, no the noo.* No simper. I was fourteen, family-fled, at home with Wee Cuddie.

Did your mother have the Gaelic? (You have it as an aura, not speak it as a function.) *Aye. Bit ma faither wouldnae hae it spoke in the hoose. He wis feart she'd gab it wi fowk, an he'd no unnerstaun. Lairnt her tae spik Scots, fur she spoke English lik a Sassenach, aw ploom-in-the-mooth.* His eyes, full of wist, got fuller.

I probed no more. There was a worm of sorrow best left to weave a nameless tangle. But it coiled round me and I followed second nature. His *Teach Yourself Gaelic*, annotated. His *Gaelic for Beginners*, thumbed raw. His *Dualchas Nàdair na h-Alba*, with marginal translations. The natural heritage of Scotland, elevated from bin to top shelf. I could reach it now, without a garrulous chair.

Kelp! Suddenly. *Luath feamnach.* Seaweed ashes. So, he did have the Gaelic. *Ah'll tell ye aboot kelp.* And he did. How it grew, how the sea cast it out, how it was gathered for lazybeds and burned for its iodine. How rich men paid poor folk to harvest it while there was a market. How poor people begged rich folk for work when there wasn't. How work songs were sung, how longing songs lingered as last chords for lost causes.

Biology, agriculture, chemistry, industry, social history, economics, music … a curriculum of conversation. *But y'ken, Ah'm no an educatit man. Ye'll lairn aw that at the skweel.* Little did he know.

Stop bletherin, there's a lav'rock tweedlin. Where (oh foolish question)? *Yer lugs is fu o haivers frae that pea-pod bit o troke! It's aboon yer heid!* I had discarded my precious new digital magic before we left the cottage. Not soon enough. I didn't tell him I'd played a bird-song track. Wrath's less raw in small doses. Aye, maybe, Grandfather.

A thocht ye cried me Wee Cuddie? Aye, but not when you sound like Dad. The lark amplified the silence. An ascending silence to a crescendo of spiralling scrutiny. Whose? His. Mine.

Aaron stretched his neck, glanced over at the quiet war, thrust his head rearward like an avian Fulton Mackay, lifted his wings as only a heron can, and drifted off. Disdain, insouciance, schadenfreude in greys with a streak of yellow. *The Irish caw it a crane bit we cry a crane a cran an, in ony case, that's Lang Sandy, an corra-ghritheach, the grey heron.* Wee Cuddie expounded restlessly, ceaselessly, in tides. *Ardea cinerea, if ye*

7

want tae ken fur real. I did, and said so. He was, in his words, *blythe, joco, cantie.* Content in mine. The battle was over.

Yer mam's no here, son. Tak a dram. A half-bottle of reproachment, rapprochement. A long arm passed it over; a short smile passed with it. Ritual. Rich ritual. Growing up rich with nature, with Wee Cuddy – and with Aaron.

Happy Families
by Maggie Rabatski

Scottish Arts Club Short Story Finalist 2014

Any minute now Cameron's going to pick up his jacket and say he's going home. I can't think of any more ways to keep him here. Colin and Pugsy went away ages ago. They're going to the movies with their Mum and Dad. Star Trek then a pizza.

We've been practising penalties in Cameron's granny's back garden all afternoon. It's brilliant for football … long and dead level, huge … no flowers or plants or trees to get in the way. His granny's a laugh. She says things like, time enough to take up gardening when I'm too old for singing and dancing, and she's 82. When she's at home she shouts us in after we've been playing a while. Grubs up she says then puts a massive plate of sandwiches on the table, all different kinds. Cheese and coleslaw's the best or beef and horseradish sauce. I never even heard of horseradish sauce before. Any drink we want as well. Tea or milk or Irn Bru or Coke and other ones I can't remember. And she always has a bowl of oranges cut into quarters, she says that's what footballers got at half-time in the olden days. She's away to Portugal for the winter, but she still lets us use the garden because it discourages burglars. She goes away every year for three months. That's how her skin's dark brown all the time.

Cameron's going over to his jacket. Five more shots I say.

Aw Kev, I need to go home. I'm starving. My Mum's making burgers tonight. My wee brother's a glutton, he'll guzzle all the second helpings if I'm late.

Go on Cam. Please. Just five more and that's it.

Why do you not like going home, Kev?

I do so. I do so like going home. It's just no time. My tea'll no be ready yet. Our tea's later than yours. That's not true but Cameron doesn't know it's not true because I'm not allowed to bring any pals into the house.

Anyway, my stepdad's a dick.

How come?

Dunno. He just is, he's just a dick.

So why did your Mum marry him if he's a dick?

How should I know? Maybe she was sick of being poor. He's got money, he's a lawyer. We used to live in a council house. That's how we moved here, moved into his house, his big house. I don't know. He was quite nice away back at the beginning.

Does your sister like him?

No way, she hates him even more than I hate him. Says he's a perv as well as a dick. Won't even stay in the same room as him. Eats her dinner in her bedroom, keeps the door locked. Says she's getting a flat soon as she's 16, she's counting the days on a calendar, a hundred to go from yesterday.

Ok *you* can have five more shots. I don't want any more. Then I'm going, definitely.

I'm going to take them good and steady, focus really hard. If I score five it's a sign everything will be ok. Or maybe just four, four out of five will be enough. Commons to take the first and last, Ledley, Stokes and Samaras for the middle three. Cameron's in position, eyes on the ball, swaying a little side to side. I'm trying to read his mind. He likes to dive to the left, but he knows I know that, so he'll probably go to the right. Or maybe he'll guess I'm thinking that and go for the left. Aw shit, forget it, I'll just batter the ball in, pretend it's his head the night he punched my mum in the stomach in front of me. Just because she told him to leave me alone. And everything goes blurry and the next thing I know I've scored five, one after another sweet as you like, and Cameron is standing there looking a bit scared.

I walk to his house with him although it's the opposite way to mine. I wish he would ask me in, but I know he won't 'cause it's Saturday. It's all happy families round here, doing special Saturday night things. I like Cameron's house. They're nice to each other. His father is nice to his mother, calls her sweetie. I like sitting there listening to them, sometimes I pretend they're my family but that's daft, so I don't do it that much. His Dad is teaching Cameron chess. I'm learning it too by watching them. He says I can have a game any time I want. His Dad is kind of quiet, doesn't say that much to me. How're you doing lad, that's about it, but you can feel it, he really wants to know. Sometimes I nearly tell him. His Mum's the opposite, always gabbing. I like her too … but I would keep my own Mum, the way she was before she met him. Now she's on another planet, dead jumpy, always cleaning the house. Doesn't even go out with her pals any more.

See you then Kev.

Aye. See you tomorrow?

Not sure about tomorrow Kev. Might have to go … I think there's some family thing on.

Ok Monday. See you.

I walk home slow as I can without looking stupid. The long way up past the Greek church. If there's nobody about I walk up and down the same road a few times before going on to the next one. You can smell dinners mixed up with the smell of gardens. Steak and chips. I'm hungry and I'm no hungry. It's like my stomach's pure empty but food isn't what it wants. I can stand being hungry for hours now. It winds him up when I'm late for my dinner. My mum says can you no come home on time to keep the peace. You know what he's like. Could you no just do it for me? I want to do it for her, but I can't get him out of my head, the way he sits there in his bigshot leather chair with his brandies and his big know-all face getting redder and redder, giving out orders and talking shite.

I'm an hour and a half late when I reach our road and I see it there, the ambulance, at our house, just moving away from our house. Oh Jesus, let it not be her. Please I'll do anything, anything … I'll never be late for my dinner ever again, please, please. Now the ambulance is passing me, and the flashing lights are on, but I can only see the driver, he's bald and he's got on black-rimmed specs. The other paramedic must be in the back, it must be serious. Serious. I'm shaking, and I can't get the key in the lock. I start banging on the door and I'm shouting let

11

me in let me in. The door opens and it's my sister and she looks different. I'm screaming where's my ma? where's my ma? what's he done to her? Anne grabs my jacket and pulls me inside. Shut up ya dumplin', my ma's ok. She's just gone to the hospital in the ambulance wi' him. He's had a heart-attack or a stroke or something … cracked his heid open on the fireplace an' aw when he collapsed.

Is he ok, is he deid?

He looked deid tae me. He wis a funny colour, the side of his face that wisnae covered in blood wis a funny colour. The paramedics were pumping away at his chest for ages …

Time to celebrate she says and goes over to the sideboard he calls the drinks cabinet and takes out a bottle. His brandy. His 'nothing but the best for the best' Martell. One time my ma brought hame a different one from the supermarket because the price was knocked down a fiver. He went off his nut. Don't bring your bargain basement mentality into this house. You're not living in a slum now. I wanted her tae smash the bottle ower his heid but she just said I'll change it tomorrow. Anne gets two tumblers, the best crystal ones out of the cupboard, puts one down beside me and pours in a little, fills it up wi lemonade then pours a big slosh for herself.

Jesus, I say, do you think we should be celebrating that he's deid, that he's maybe deid. I know he's a dick but I mean is it no going a bit far … I mean, it might be bad luck.

Anne is sitting in his chair, leg-rest up and everything. I've never seen anyone sitting on that chair but him, never. Ooooh listen to you, Mr Sensitivity all of a sudden, she says. Ok well, Ah suppose if it makes you feel better *you* can just drink to being rid of the bastard for wan hale heavenly Saturday night. Cheers!

Ralph by
Andy Frazier

Scottish Arts Club Short Story Finalist 2014

Tony watched the fat grey bird with mild disdain as it hopped from yellow foot to yellow foot, inching its way across the damp grass. What was it with seagulls that made them so undesirable? Rats with wings, someone had once described them. A slither of paper, possibly a sweet wrapper, was the object of this one's attention, lying on a patch of damp sandy dirt under the wooden bench. With little consideration, Tony put his foot over it, the worn tread of his walking boot obscuring it from view, and then glanced out over the estuary.

Faint lines of distant white waves rose and fell from the dappled surface, as though raising their heads and then lowering them again like meerkats peeking out to see if the coast is clear.

Across the bay, two identical hills loomed from the otherwise darkening skies over Fife. It must be nearly two years that he had been coming here to this bench, and yet still he hadn't gotten around to finding out what they were called. The Queen's nipples, he always referred to them as, due to their shape with a pimple on top, like a woman lying topless on a chilly beach. The Royal reference was to Fife itself, known quite boastfully as the Kingdom of Fife as though a powerful King owned it personally. Well a king had a queen, didn't it? And its queen was right there, lying on her back. Tony had never really discussed this with anyone; people didn't like that sort of thing when it came to nudity and royalty. And anyway, since Laura had gone, he didn't much talk to anybody else. At first, he had tried to be brave, and even ventured down to the Bissets pub on the main street and chatted with John behind the bar; but it wasn't really conversation, just talk, pretend to listen, and then wait for your turn to talk again. He had an idea the few locals laughed about him when he left. After a couple of visits, he got bored with it – and them – and got a dog instead.

By his foot, the grey bird had got nearer and was now inspecting the area where his boot was. He glanced down at it, staring into its shiny eye. For a second, it reminded him of Ralph, and the way that he had always looked at him with that expectant expression when he wanted something.

"Oh Ralph," he sighed. "Why did you leave too?"

"Ralph!" squawked the feathered creature, its beak open at right-angles.

Tony let out an involuntary laugh. Ralph had been called Ralph as a joke, because when he barked it sounded just like that very word. The dog was a walking onomatopoeic creature that would be a sketch-writers dream.

"Ralph! Ralph!" he said out loud, to no one in particular.

The bird glanced down at his foot, repeated his words in its birdlike tone, and then pecked at his boot.

"Are you mocking me, you scavenging beast?" Tony raised his foot to push it away, but the bird ducked its head underneath it and snatched the sweet wrapper like a well-practised pickpocket. He watched it back away, hanging on to the white paper so that it didn't take off on the breeze, and then turned his eyes back out over the dunes to the sea once more. Out in the bay a giant oil tanker sat empty and motionless, its red whale-like body sitting high up out of the water and exposing its lower waistline like an old man's sock at half-mast. As usual, it wasn't the boat or the water that interested Tony, but the thicket of gorse and buckthorn that smothered the rolling hills of sand for the quarter of a mile or so between him and Gullane beach. To the left it extended back towards Edinburgh, culminating with the massive old house that towered over the golf course, backlit against the afternoon sky. He had searched there, so many times. Out to his right, sprawling eastwards towards the North Sea and past Muirfield course, the dense buckthorn gave way to spindly pine trees that flailed and thrashed in the wind on blowy days.

It was there, within a stone's throw of the second green, that he had last seen poor Ralph.

That had been over a month ago.

Each morning, at first light, Tony had checked outside the door of his tiny house in Broadgait, in case he had come home during the night, returning after a frantic scurry around in the undergrowth, momentarily forgetting the time or day. Each morning, the heartache wrenched at Tony's soul, like a sucker punch to the stomach. With every morning, the hope grew thinner until now it was barely more than a distant wish. Time was healing, just like they said it would, but as the optimism faded so it gave way to an emptiness that was filled with scalding pain.

"Are you still out there, Ralph?" His eyes scanned back and forth, pulling a pair of field-glasses tight into his sockets like his old tank commander had done in the dusty desert.

Since Laura had left him over a year ago, that scruffy dog had been his only friend; and, in a short time, they had been through immeasurable emotional turmoil together. Late into the night, he would sit and hold perfectly acceptable conversations with him, while the dog sat and listened patiently about life with all its horrors, prospects and values. Occasionally, when he understood words like birdies or sausages, he would chip in with a few of his own. Ralph, Ralph.

Tony considered that it was everyone's wish that their dog could talk. Or their cat, or hamster? On patrol, one scary night, he had even talked to a lizard while, somewhere inside him, willing it to talk back to him in words he could understand. Just a few words of encouragement – that was all he needed? Well, that's what made Ralph so special. He did that.

Tony surveyed the land again, casting his eyes across the thorny bushes, their once bright orange berries fading like forgotten Christmas decorations, as winter turned its head towards springtime. A young couple on the distant beach were throwing a ball for their own dog, adding pain and guilt to the thoughts he already harboured, about what he once had, now all gone.

"But gone, it is!" he sighed, addressing the obese bird as it watched him, now perched on a gnarled wooden fence.

"Ralph!" squawked the bird again, but this time, to Tony's surprise, opening its wings and swooping the ten feet or so towards him. As he flinched, it stuck out its claws, heavily thudding onto the back-rest of the bench and balancing there, the green wooden rail bending fractionally under its weight. Still in slight shock, he watched it fold its wings up like a child's transformer toy, tucking them away until it resumed its rotund shape once more. Resisting the urge to chase the seagull away, Tony turned towards it, admiring the intricate array of dark and light feathers that together made up its grey appearance. Still wary it may attack him, he spoke to it again.

"Have you seen Ralph, my friend?" he asked, quietly. "Is he out there, chasing birdies like you, and causing menace?" As he stared at it, tears uncontrollably welling up in his eyes, the bird fixed his gaze once more. "Is he out there now, running free?" Tony swallowed hard. "Or maybe up there?" He broke the animal's stare and looked up to the grey skies overhead, where a few clouds were assembling like a gathering army of grey wool-sacks. "Do you think he will come back, some day?" When he glanced back down, the bird was looking up too, following his gaze.

"Ralph," it said, much quieter this time. Then there was nothing, except the silence of nature's own background.

For the first time in weeks, Tony felt his pain drain away as his lips slowly widened to a smile. Their eyes locked again as its pupils, jet black against pools of vibrant yellow, seemed to peer into his soul. His heart quickened, and the young man felt his voice drop to a whisper.

"You can understand me, can't you? You know, don't you? You know all about Ralph?"

Using slow movements, he delved his cold hand into the depths of his coat pocket, burrowing beneath a mass of tissues before bringing out a small plastic bag. He tore open the top and offered a brown object in the palm of his outstretched hand.

"Are you a smart birdie?" His voice raised in encouragement. "Do you like sausages?"

"Ralph! Ralph!" came the eager reply.

The Road to Success
by Alli Sangster-Wall

Scottish Arts Club Short Story Finalist 2014

Kathryn McQuirk looked out nervously to the cabaret tables surrounding the stage, the dim lights making it difficult to discern individual eager faces. The central lamps cast shadows on the features of the audience turning them into sinister gargoyles. She looked down at the award in her hands, the coveted prize for short fiction, gripping it tightly to stop her hands from shaking; a heady cocktail of nerves at the prospect of meeting the mystery scribe and withdrawal.

The MC, Bob Barrett, Chairman of the Literary Society, was giving the usual spiel, describing the great writer of mysteries and crime fiction, a leader in the genre, one of Britain's literary guiding lights. Kathryn felt the knot in her stomach tighten. They would know the truth soon enough; they would know how unworthy of their praise she truly was. She quickly slipped the hand-written note from her pocket underneath the trophy.

Those interminable days of judging short stories had been spent alternately cursing her agent for volunteering her for the panel and feeling distinctly underwhelmed at the trotted-out clichés, standard tales of romance and predictable mysteries that passed over her desk. Judging this competition was punishment for her vices. A recent appearance on BBC Breakfast where she had promoted her latest DI Ross novel through slurred words and glazed eyes had caused widespread talk of addiction and dependency. She needed a good news story to take the heat off, her agent said, worried about his percentage if her new novel bombed. The quality of her writing was coming under fire – a convincing alcoholic detective didn't seem such a clever feat of fiction when it was written by an alcoholic writer.

Reaching for the next script, she took a good slug of gin. I don't have a problem, she thought, I could stop anytime I wanted, if I wanted, I only drink socially, I'm sure my husband is in the house somewhere this evening, equally sloshed. The latest story piqued her interest instantly, grabbing her attention with its vivid description of a neighbourhood she knew well. She stood from her office chair, stretched out and moved across to the leather Chesterfield, sitting down and curling her legs underneath her. This story was worthy of her full attention.

It was a dark night, raining heavily, the action beginning on one of the tree-lined streets in the nicer part of town; a familiar setting. A man in his forties was walking his dog. Bound to find a body, Kathryn had guessed, they always do. A young woman was walking on the opposite side of the wide street, coming towards the man and his dog. She was wearing a red anorak, too light a coat for the time of year. Kathryn's mind ran ahead, will the young woman be the victim then, witnessing the crime would be an infinitely more interesting prospect for the dog walker. She found herself intrigued by the story, the writing drawing her in; the first among the manuscripts that had achieved that effect. It's the familiarity, she thought, I care because I know the area, it's described so well. Suddenly a car screamed into the road, struggling to regain traction from the erratic turn made on two wheels. It was a sports car, soft top, rear wheel drive, careering on the damp road surface. Then that extra detail – the car was a classic Mercedes 280SL – in silver.

Kathryn's glass slipped from her hand, the crystal shattering, sending ice cubes skidding across the wooden floor. She sat up, gripping the edges of the pages, the words swimming in front of her. That car, her prized possession, bought when her first DI Ross novel had been reprinted for the third time, a runaway success. The purchase of that beautiful car heralded a short-lived period of self-congratulation, she had achieved her dreams; she was published and successful and she was reaping the rewards until that night. She was suddenly back there, feeling the leather of the steering wheel beneath her right hand as she gripped it to lean over and retrieve her cigarettes from her handbag on the passenger seat. The wheel turned with her as she leaned, the bump of the kerb jarring her as her eyes took a moment to pull the scene back into focus. She corrected sharply, pulling down on the wheel just as the young woman stepped out from the opposite side of the road. A bang, a flash of red anorak, no more, then the car moving off as Kathryn stamped her heel heavily on the accelerator instead of the brake and didn't stop, the wheels spinning as she drove off screaming into the night. That small forgotten detail was remembered now in vivid horror; she had glanced into the rear-view mirror and seen the woman in red on the ground, crumpled at the side of the road and, stood over her, a man with his dog.

As a blackmail note it was ingenious. Nobody knew about that night, other than Kathryn herself and, it would seem, the amateur writer. There was no accompanying note, no demands made; the story had been submitted through the official channel amongst the sea of others. Yet it was unmistakably a threat. If awarded the first prize the story would become public, but as a work of fiction. Kathryn could only assume that if it was not awarded the prize it may very well become public as an account of fact. She had thought many times about that night, about the woman in the red anorak. She had scoured the local papers for weeks afterwards, waiting for the story to be covered, willing it to be an account of the young woman's survival and recovery rather than an appeal for witnesses to a murder. It had never appeared in the local or national news, and the damage to her car had been the only thing that kept Kathryn from convincing herself that it had not really happened, a figment of her intoxicated imagination, a spectre of events yet to come if she continued down her path of self-destruction. But the car had been damaged; a large dent and smashed headlight, and there, caught on the glass, a shred of red material. Weeks later Kathryn had burnt the car, set it alight in the garage one night and claimed it on her insurance, unable to bear the sight of it anymore. It had no longer represented her success, only her failings.

The MC, Bob Barrett, was finished with the lavish introduction and now extended his right arm to the side of the stage beckoning Kathryn to join him at the lectern. She was frozen to the spot; Bob looked pointedly at her and repeated her name before somebody behind her gave her a gentle nudge in the back to get her moving. She hesitantly wandered onto the stage, looking out at the tables in awe. Bob watched, bemused, as Kathryn approached; looking to be suffering from an acute case of stage fright. He had seen her speak publicly before, a consummate professional and confident orator, but then again, he had also seen that BBC Breakfast slot and had been aware she was a gamble as head judge this year. Bob took a couple of steps forward and reached out his hand to Kathryn, reeling her in to position behind the microphone. She cleared her throat several times before, with her voice shaking, she began to read the winning entry, a public confession disguised as fiction. As she got lost in the catharsis her voice gained strength and the audience listened, enthralled, to the words read with such raw emotion by McQuirk. Bob watched, nodding along at the side of stage – this was the impressive lady he remembered, holding the audience rapt as she weaved the story, her vocal inflections creating atmosphere for the dark tale of a hit and run.

Kathryn stood looking down at the prize in her hands, steeling herself. Time to face the man who would blackmail her, who had witnessed the crime and had waited, biding his time, until this opportunity to make her atone had presented itself. He would leave £5000 richer that night, but Kathryn knew this would only be the beginning; he would come back for more now that he knew she would capitulate.

"And so, onto the Award. The 2014 National Literary Society prize for short fiction is awarded to G. A. Allerton." The audience applauded enthusiastically as Kathryn made the announcement, scanning the room for movement. For a long moment nobody stood up. The clapping started to falter as people looked around, seeking the winner, whispering amongst themselves. The applause petered out entirely then the silence was broken by the scrape of a chair being pushed back. All eyes turned to see a woman in a red dress stand and walk purposefully towards the stage and her prize.

The Instructions of Miss Mary Jones
by David Mathews

Scottish Arts Club Short Story Finalist 2014

Bryncleddau, Wednesday

Dear Mr Rowlands

As I see from the newsletter that you are still churchwarden, may I ask you a slightly out-of-the-ordinary favour? You were so kind when I last came to church – all the trouble you went to. Your wife too, when I telephoned that day last spring and kept her talking for hours. I am usually so brief on the phone.

I have known for several years that I shall not live very long. I only get about near my house now. Fortunately, there are a few shops nearby and my neighbour is very good, coming in most days. My nephew Ian pops over from Swansea when he can, but that is not very often because his wife seems so busy.

My illness is strange. I feel bad only on certain days, but it drags me down constantly. When I am feeling well, I worry about how I will be when I wake next morning. Dr Tom is charming, I must say, but rather flippant. Miss Jones, he says, you will be with us a long time yet. He says he can find nothing wrong with me. When I go, he will be surprised, and I am only sorry that I will not have the satisfaction of hearing him admit that I was right after all.

Unfortunately, of course, my doctor's refusal to take seriously how ill I am means that he is unlikely to be alert enough to give me decent notice of my demise, which is why I have been thinking again about where my ashes will be buried. I now owe you an apology. Despite all the rigmarole you went through to have a plot reserved for me in the churchyard, I wish to relinquish it in order to have my ashes scattered with my mother's among the roses at Thornhill. Do you think, nevertheless, that your nice vicar would still take my funeral? Would you ask her for me?

21

As to what happens in the service, I have lodged my instructions with the Co-op undertakers. I have said, of course, that I wish my funeral to be at St Thomas. I have chosen two hymns – *Love Divine*, the merrier tune (is it *Hyfrydol* or the *Stainer*?), and *Aberystwyth*. For a reading, I have chosen Jesus's meeting with the Samaritan woman at the well. It's unusual for a funeral, this story of an immoral woman and a foreigner to boot, but I hope you will shortly understand why I have chosen it. Would your wife consider reading it?

I want no eulogy. Ian will object no doubt, but please ask your vicar to be firm on this. I am not an especially keen follower of funerals, unlike some of my neighbours, and I find that the eulogy so often diminishes the person. I do not wish to be remembered as the object of an embarrassing recital of trivia.

Please can someone ring the bell for me as I leave the church? The one I think they call the tenor would be suitably sombre. There's something proper about a single bell. It is one of the few sounds these days that makes people stop in their tracks, don't you think? I like too the idea of the physical exertion that ringing requires, and on the same theme of physicality, I have asked that my coffin be carried, not wheeled about like Tesco shopping.

I mentioned to my neighbour the other day that I was writing to you about this, and she thought it odd. How can you think of all that, she said, it's all so gloomy and depressing? As I tried to explain to her, I worry so much less about things once I have organised them.

Now, my main decision. I shall go to the crematorium alone. I have thought long and hard about this. I have been to cremations often enough to know that I do not like them, however much I recognise them as a necessity. Probably you will get my drift when I say that I do not look forward to going to the crem. I know that I will be quite unconscious of the event when it occurs, but the knowledge that it will happen irks me. Therefore, I wish to manage it the best I can. I like the idea that no one will watch in tears as the curtains draw round my coffin, nor will anyone be in anguish or confusion because they are not in tears. It is something I can spare them.

When I say alone, I am not being strictly accurate. I mean that I would like you to be my sole companion apart from the undertakers. No Ian, no family, no vicar. Will you do that for me? I do not need you to say anything – apart from a few words I shall mention in a moment. No-one will be listening, least of all me, but I would be grateful to have the reassurance of what I might call your oversight. No disrespect to the good men and women at the crem, nor to those at the Co-op, but I am sure they do not get through their working day without a measure of dark humour. This is utterly understandable, and I would be the same in their place. I would value your presence, therefore, as ensuring a certain decorum. You seemed quite unperturbed to talk to me about death when you guided me through the arrangements before, so perhaps you might like to finish the job, if I may put it that way.

I confess to being anxious about the process of dying. It could be painful or drawn out, it could be undignified. At my age it is unlikely to be violent, though that was not always so. It may be deeply poignant, for I might feel that ache of things not done and of never again doing those things that bear repeating. I am less worried than I once was about the state of being dead, for all that priests would have us be anxious about it and explain our anxiety as a fear of hell. Sir Thomas Browne understood our condition all that time ago, when what he said was, 'The long habit of living indisposeth us for dying'. Have you read him?

There is another reason I wish to go to the crem alone. You know me as Miss Jones, or Mary. Those are not my real names. When I left school I was 15 – just before Neville Chamberlain went to Munich. During the war I had a job as a typist, and with my friends had an exciting time being entertained by young men trying to live out their hazardous lives intensely or pretending to. When the war ended, everything changed, and those of us who had been loving and generous to frightened soldiers were now characterised as 'easy' or 'tarts'. I fell into a difficult marriage – it would now be called abusive – dominated by jealousy, drink and too little money left over. I had a baby girl, but nothing changed. One Friday night when my husband took drunken exception to my asking for money and beat me yet again, I stabbed him with a kitchen knife. I was not the first to do such a thing, but in shock I took to my bed and by the time my husband's workmates came looking for him on the Monday, my little girl was also dead.

At my trial, it was the death of my daughter from neglect that was counted the greater crime. I cannot dissent from that view, though I do not feel that the culprit was me. I was jailed for manslaughter amid raucous cheers from the popular press. When I was released, my mother and I changed our names and we moved to Cardiff. In time I obtained a job in the Central Library. Ian is the son of my neighbour in Bryncleddau; I became 'Auntie Mary' to him and he became my 'nephew'. He knows no details of my early history, another reason to steer clear of a eulogy – no need for him to delve.

My special request is this. At the crematorium I wish you, at the very end, to pronounce my real name and that of my daughter. I am content to know that you will stand there and say, 'So and so, loving mother of baby … goodbye.' Just that. The Co-op have the names you will need in a sealed envelope among my other instructions.

Please give my best wishes to your wife. I love listening to her voice. If you agree my request, I am happy for you to tell her about it, but only her please.

With kindest regards

Mary Jones (Miss)

The Tale of Penelope Cupcake
by Ruth Howell

Winner, Scottish Arts Club Short Story Competition 2015

People said the oddest things to Penelope Cupcake.

"Have you always been overweight?" they asked.

"Over *what* weight?" she would reply, for she walked lightly, like a cat, and she knew for certain that her footprints were no deeper than anyone else's.

On the day she moved into Orchard Cottage, Penelope wandered between the ancient fruit trees, where the pears and apples hung heavily from the branches and rejoiced in their abundance. Her village friends had wished her well. "And of course, you'll have the Gingerbreads next door, Teddy and Serena. Such a glamorous couple, the Gingerbreads."

However, standing on Serena's doorstep that first morning, a basket of freshly-baked muffins on her arm, Penelope saw that she and Serena were not destined to be friends. Serena's front door disturbed her; in its bevelled glass she saw herself splintered into shrapnel, transformed into a hard-edged puzzle. The doorbell tinkled. A smiling Serena appeared. Her gaze took several moments longer than necessary to circumscribe Penelope's outline, and the hand she extended felt, in Penelope's, like a bundle of sticks. In the hallway beyond Serena, one wall was taken up entirely by a studio portrait of the Gingerbreads.

"What a delightful photo," Penelope said politely.

"Oh, that," Serena gave a little laugh. "Isn't Teddy adorable?"

Penelope stared at the photo of Teddy Gingerbread. Those eyes … goodness! That look was positively indecent! It wasn't sex, exactly. No, it was far more dangerous than that. It looked very much like hunger.

Serena led the way through the house. A flat light glared from every surface. They stepped through the kitchen and onto a patio; in a large swimming pool a pair of arms, rigid and mechanical, chopped through the air like propeller blades. Serena poured coffee from a tiny cafetière. Penelope noted an absence of biscuits.

"It's a wonderful neighbourhood," Serena was saying. "There's so much to do: tennis, combat aerobics, yoga, tai chi …"

"Coffee mornings?" Penelope asked.

The cafetière faltered. "Oh, no," Serena said. "No coffee mornings."

At that moment Teddy sprang from the pool and began to towel himself dry. "Teddy darling," Serena called. "Come and meet Penelope. She's just moved in next door."

Teddy turned. Penelope noted the sculpted torso, the perfect musculature. Teddy looked at Penelope, then at Serena, then back again, as if considering whether the girth of Penelope's upper arm might exactly equal that of Serena's slender thigh. "Hello, Penelope," he said. Penelope looked into his eyes. Yes, there it was.

Hunger. How extraordinary. "Hello, Teddy."

Penelope placed her basket on the table. Beneath the checked red cloth, the muffins nestled and shifted, steaming gently.

Serena lifted the cloth and peeked into the basket. Her mouth twisted.

"Oh," she said. "Muffins."

In an instant, Teddy's hand was in the basket. Serena lunged, slapping swiftly. "No, Teddy! Naughty!"

Teddy withdrew, nursing his hand against his naked chest. He looked at Penelope. Penelope looked back.

After fifteen awkward minutes, Penelope was once more on Serena's doorstep. "Well, goodbye," Serena said, a little stiffly. "And do take your … *muffins*." She handed over Penelope's basket and closed the door. Penelope stood quite still. Poor Serena; how she pitied her. But not as much as she pitied Teddy. Back at Orchard Cottage, Penelope threw open her cupboards. A restorative was required; something aromatic, she felt. Cinnamon and cloves, perhaps. Apples, and the lightest shortcrust pastry.

She weighed, she measured; only when her creation was safely bedded in the oven, melting into golden perfection, did she rest. As the heady aroma filled her kitchen, she opened her windows and filled Orchard Lane with the scent of happiness.

It was almost midnight when she went to bed. She placed the remains of her creation by the open kitchen window. As she turned off the light, something rustled in the shrubbery. A cat, perhaps. Penelope smiled to herself. A cat that looked remarkably like Teddy.

In the morning, Penelope was gratified to see her pie-dish licked clean. When Teddy and Serena jogged past as usual at six thirty, their arms swinging in unison, Penelope sighed. Poor Teddy! He always looked so exhausted, so unhappy. He was, she suspected, a true creature of appetite, a thwarted colossus of gaping button and straining belt. Oh, what a man he might be, released from the bondage of that muscled corset, that sculpted armour!

But Teddy's crime had been discovered, it seemed. Serena was alert to further lapses for, after that first success, Penelope's offerings on the windowsill went untouched. One evening, as Teddy walked homewards, shambling along the lane like an animated mop, his tummy rumbled audibly. It was too much; Penelope lifted a tray of madeleines and stepped outside.

"Good evening, Teddy," she said. "Are you ... hungry?"

Teddy turned his weary eyes to her, to the madeleines, and inhaled deeply. He still felt cheated by the muffins. His tummy gave another gurgle as he thought of the tofu salad waiting for him in the fridge. It was Serena's Pilates night.

Penelope set the tray down on her little garden table. Teddy was looking a trifle unsteady so she helped him into a chair. She gestured to the tray. "Can I tempt you? I've been baking all day." Slumped in the chair, Teddy gazed at her in wonder. "You have *baking* days?"

Penelope smiled. "Goodness, no. *Every* day is a baking day."

Teddy looked at the pastries and began to cry. "I mustn't," he said. "Serena will kill me." The sour scent of starvation was rolling off him in waves. Penelope patted his hand.

"I often make too much. So, if I left out a little something, now and then, there wouldn't be any harm in that, surely?"

And there in front of her, on her little garden chair, Teddy broke apart like an overcooked meringue. His life was a sham, he confessed. He was tormented by fantasies of the darkest kind; of enormous dinner-lady arms, poised above vast urns of steaming custard, ladling over trays of spotted dick.

Penelope was shocked; shocked and thrilled. She took his hand in hers, "You mustn't feel ashamed, Teddy. These are perfectly natural desires."

A new phase began. Each evening Penelope left a little something on the windowsill, and each evening the little something disappeared. No words were said but, from time to time, a trail of crumbs was discernible, leading out through the gate and down the lane.

Serena took to jogging alone. Teddy was ill, she said, but in truth she was too embarrassed to be seen with him. He was expanding at an alarming rate, bursting out of his Lycra in several places. She put him on a strict diet of carrot sticks and bean sprouts.

Friends visited, bringing Penelope all the gossip of the village. Serena was distraught, it seemed. Teddy was not himself. For a start, he was absurdly happy. Something Was Going On. Teddy's attention had wandered. But where could it have gone, Serena wailed. There was no-one slimmer, fitter, neater, flatter than Serena Gingerbread.

Week after week, Penelope busied herself in her kitchen, turning out fondants, mousses, gateaux. Serena now jogged past four times a day, her bony knees pumping the air. Goodness, Penelope thought. How *thin* she was getting. She was positively translucent. Before long, she was compelled to run with a dumb-bell in each hand, in case a strong gust of wind carried her off.

Over the months, Penelope watched as Teddy expanded. It was a joy to see him lurking in the hedge, eyeing up her windowsill. Now and then she rewarded him with a special treat. On the day she spied his Lycra shorts in the dustbin, she let rip with a volley of chocolate éclairs.

But, oh, how Serena suffered. These days, people could hear her coming, for her head had become a pale skull with her teeth rattling around inside like cherry stones. Penelope felt a little guilty. At first, she'd been aware only of Teddy's misery; she'd simply wanted to help. But now, as he ballooned, she found herself thrilled by his corpulence. Nothing happened, of course, for the bonds of marriage were sacrosanct. She was quite old-fashioned that way.

And then, one day, the inevitable happened. A tearful Teddy arrived at Penelope's door with dreadful news. He'd embraced Serena, quite fondly, and she'd snapped in two like a twig.

The funeral was a quiet affair. Serena was borne aloft in a coffin of butterfly wings, which was tethered down, during the service, with her dumb-bells.

Penelope, sitting in an uncomfortably narrow pew, dabbed her eyes. Poor Serena. There was nothing anyone could have done to help her.

That evening, as the sun was setting, Penelope took her special heart-shaped tin from the fridge and turned out her masterpiece, the Coeur à la Crème, garnished with tiny caramelised strawberries. She stood for a moment, admiring the heart in all its perfection. Then, with a little sigh of pleasure, she settled down to wait.

I'm Not on the Tram
by Helen Morris

Scottish Arts Club Short Story Finalist 2015

Tam eased his arm carefully out from under her warm body and tentatively emerged from the cocoon of the duvet. He picked up his phone from the bedside table and tiptoed out of the bedroom. It was five o'clock in the morning and, being early March in Edinburgh, still pitch-black outside. Tam stumbled into the sitting room and was just about to install himself on the settee when he noticed a mound of blankets and remembered their pal Percy had crashed out the night before rather than face the uphill cycle home.

He had no choice but to make the unheated kitchen his centre of operations. He pulled on an old Aran jumper and some jeans and mismatched socks and sitting at the table, his feet propped against the opposite chair, he typed in the address of the online auction site. It was less than an hour before the auction ended. Six in the morning was certainly a curious time to pick for the bids to end but the seller was in Australia where presumably it was a much more sensible time of day. Offline, Tam checked the Wi-Fi on his phone, switched on but no signal. No need to panic, he grabbed the tablet, nothing, the old laptop held together with Duck Tape, no signal. He checked the modem; the light was red and solid. He yanked the plug out of the wall, counted one thousand, two thousand … thirty thousand, power on, still nothing. OK backup plan, internet café, library. Not at 5 a.m.

There had to be internet somewhere in the city. The cooker clock showed 0511. Tam slapped his forehead with the palm of his hand. Of course, the tram! First departure, York Place 0529.

He stole quietly back into the sitting room and carefully lifted Percy's keys off the floor. He headed out of the flat door, down the tenement stair and out onto the still icy street.

Percy's bike was locked to the railings, the long chain lovingly intertwined around the wheels, frames and fence. There were two distinct frames expertly – at least Tam hoped they were – welded together. Percy's great-great grandfather, a schoolmaster in Kegworth, had joined what had once been two tandems into a magnificent quad bike. Speeding around the hairpin bends of Nottinghamshire on a Friday after school had helped him blow off steam after another week battling with the school board.

Tam had only ever been a passenger on the contraption while Percy steered but it hadn't looked that hard, at least not from where he had been sitting. At this hour of the morning Easter Road was mercifully clear of traffic and only a couple of food delivery vans pulled out in front of him as he turned into London Road. He safely negotiated the roundabout at the top of Leith Walk by crouching low and tilting the quad in what Tam felt was the style of a TT racer, past the Playhouse and around the final roundabout he saw the tram pulling into the stop. His plan was going to succeed! The Edinburgh Trams Customer Service agent hovered in the vehicle doorway and Tam fished into his pocket for money to buy the ticket.

No wallet! A trickle of cold sweat ran down his back.

He patted his pockets desperately but, no money, only his phone. He quickly connected to the tram Wi-Fi and found the auction. The price was still within his budget; he would just have to hope the last-minute bidders were slower than him.

Clang, clang the doors closed and the tram trundled off along York Place. Tam leapt back on the quad, balanced the phone in one hand and steered with the other, just managing to stay in touch with the Wi-Fi signal but had no free hand to refresh the screen and see how the auction was going. The phone half slid out of his hand as he turned the bike past the Portrait Gallery and pedalled uphill to St Andrew Square. The incline wasn't steep but with only one hand on the handlebars and a gearless bike made for four, Tam was struggling to keep up with the tram. 'Have youse nae pals?' A couple of squaddies looking like they were on their way back from a night out, yelled at Tam from the gardens in the middle of the square.

"Gisa shot."

"Help me pedal?" Tam said hopefully.

The lads lurched onto the back of the bike and began to pedal. The tram headed down the hill to Princes Street. Tam now had more power but as the squaddies whooped and hollered from the back, a lot less stability. Where was their commanding officer when you needed him?

The tram paused at the Princes Street lights and Tam took the time to hit refresh and confirm the auction was still on course. As they passed the Overseas Club a woman dressed in pilot's uniform stepped briskly out onto the pavement. She caught Tam's eye and taking in his unruly crew couldn't resist slinging her bag across her shoulders and jumping onto the last seat from where Tam could hear her barking brisk orders at the hapless squaddies to pedal fast and in an orderly fashion. With the power and order behind him Tam was easily able to keep up with the Wi-Fi signal as the tram pondered along the tranquil streets.

"I'll need to leave you at Haymarket," the pilot yelled to Tam. "I've a plane to catch. The passengers get upset if I'm late for work."

"Aye nae bother. Thanks for your help."

Tam was feeling quite relaxed as they all headed into Shandwick Place. He used the West End stop as a chance to shake out his fingers which had become cramped clutching the phone over the top of the handle bar.

As they approached Haymarket, Tam was getting ready to say goodbye and thanks to his pilot when he noticed that the tram tracks dipped down and away from the road. As the pilot stepped onto the tram with a smile and a wave, the doors closed and the vehicle, rapidly picking up speed, disappeared.

Tam hung his head and felt his spirits plummet as his great scheme had come to nought. He signalled to the squaddies to turn the quad around, trying to cross the tracks at a right angle as instructed by the man from the Council.

Clang, clang.

"Hey, hey," the squaddies cheered as the York Place bound tram arrived at the stop. They were back on.

As the unstable, but no less enthusiastic, trio chased the tram back along Princes Street, Tam put in his first bid. Immediately it was beaten. He waited a couple more minutes watching the clock on his phone until he was sure it was the last 15 seconds of the auction. As the tram and the quad with only three men sped back down North St Andrew Street, he bid again. *Auction over.*

Congratulations! You have won!

"Ya beauty!" Tam raised both arms in the air, looked skywards and closed his eyes, victorious. The quad had picked up speed on the downhill and now, without its driver to steer it around the corner to York Place, was heading straight for Dublin Street. The side of the front wheel clipped the bollards at the top of the street, the force of the impact was too much for the elderly bike, one quad became two tandems, Tam and the squaddies flew in different directions, part of the frame skidded down the cobbled street, the wheel still spinning in the air as it came to rest beside an elderly red Honda.

On the other side of the street in the gutter a mobile phone beeped, *congratulations on winning the auction for an antique engagement ring. The seller will be in touch to arrange secure delivery.*

Freight Train, Going so Fast
by Michael Hamish Glen

Scottish Arts Club Short Story Finalist 2015,
Scottish Arts Club Member's Award Winner 2015

Fran booted up his tablet and Googled for the song that kept coming back to him; the Peter, Paul and Mary version. He had forgotten that the inimitable Joan Baez had also recorded it. The second surprise was seeing that it was written back in 1905 by someone called Elizabeth Cotten. To add to his discoveries, he read that Joan Baez's mother came from Edinburgh.

The song brought back many memories of childhood, living in Lanarkshire next to the busy railway used by long goods trains that rumbled past in the middle of the night. Despite all the lorries on the roads, the bulky cars and flat-bed wagons behind the powerful locomotives still carried the 'stuff', as he used to call it, past a house he no longer lived in.

On this holiday in France, he arrived in the evening at Carcassonne on a *TER* train from Toulouse. He stepped down from the carriage just seconds before a dusty, thrusting freight train, full of fruit and vegetables from Spain, thundered through the station. *Freight train, freight train going so fast*, he sang to himself. Up till then, he'd never considered who wrote the words; that's was why he'd determined to find out.

He had booked a room – with *Wi-Fi* – at the *l'Hôtel du Soleil le Terminus*, the splendid *Beaux Arts* establishment near the *Canal du Midi*. It retained its aesthetic opulence from the early 1900s despite the little restaurant along the pavement outside. So many French towns have an *Hôtel le Terminus* but this one was special.

He checked in at the high desk in the soaring atrium, so large that the huge scattered sofas seemed insignificant. He remembered the grand staircase, palace-like corridors and sturdy bedroom doors from his last visit and was delighted that his room had a view of the *Square*

André Chénier. Was the poet 'square' too? *This is a treat,* he murmured. *Expensive, but what the hell. I won't be here forever.*

It was no prediction; it was a promise. A commitment. Fran, Francis Xavier MacMorran from birth, had run, as he liked to put it, his course. He had not even questioned the consultant who, supported by evidence of Fran's out-of-control malignant tumour, signed his death warrant.

"I can't guarantee you more than a few weeks," he said and paused, waiting for Fran's reaction. There was none. "And no, it's inoperable. Or, at least, it's operable but the result would be fatal. I wouldn't even contemplate it."

Fran remained apparently unmoved. "In which case, I'd better take that holiday in France I was planning. Thanks for being honest. It's just one more on my long list of 'nearlies'."

Hugh Summerville, the consultant, looked at him, his expression querying what Fran had said.

"I've nearly made old age," he explained. "I'm one of Scotland's nearly men. The guys who get their fingertips on the mountain top before slipping down. Like William Wallace, Bonnie Prince Charlie …" He dropped his head briefly before looking at Hugh.

"Where do you want me to start?" He got no reaction. "I nearly got a good degree, I nearly got a top job, I nearly made a success of my marriage – and of my children. I nearly got my novel published, nearly fell in love again, nearly learnt to speak French fluently."

Hugh smiled and spoke quietly. "In that case, why don't you start on the last one and enjoy your holiday at the same time. It's nearly time for your singular achievement – the ultimate conclusion."

"No hint of compassion there," said Fran. "Thanks. I'll park the self-pity and get on a plane to Paris. I really want to see the re-vamped Picasso Museum and the brilliant Citroën showroom. It was nearly open when I last visited."

And so, he tidied his house, made sure his papers were as much in order as he could be bothered and left a key with neighbours, telling them if anything happened to call his lawyer, Bernie Cowan, who would know what to do. He explained nothing – although he nearly did.

Paris was a blur of trying to do too much in too little time. He revisited the Rodin museum with its magnificent *Burghers of Calais* and the *Thinker*. He wandered down the *Champs Élysées* to see Manuelle Gautrand's electrifying showroom with its equally exhilarating concept Citroëns. At a matching, breath-taking cost, he lingered outside over a lunch of scrambled egg with smoked salmon, two glasses of wine and a double espresso. *I won't do this again in a hurry*, he smiled. *In fact, I won't do it again.*

He nearly slept, alone in a first-class four-berth sleeper, all the way to Toulouse where he re-visited the towering mediaeval Basilique St Sernin. He was an atheist with a perverse affection for this great brick Romanesque monument with its battered stone pillars inside. It had offered him inspiration (divine intervention?) when trying to compose a eulogy for a dead friend whose funeral was two hours away. "Norman was a great cathedral of a man," were his opening words and there was nearly a round of applause in the crematorium.

That was his funeral, Fran quipped. *There's no one to say that of me. Maybe, Fran was nearly a great achiever.*

A memorable evening meal followed by a glass or two of Calva (even this far south) put paid to further introspection. *Carpe diem*, or in this case, *noctem*. He'd have liked to seize something a little more corporeal but there were no candidates, so he slept the sleep of the virtuous under an expensive duvet.

And so on to Carcassonne, a place where he felt 'comfortable'. On his first visit one summer, he had emerged from Ryanair's conditioned air into a cauldron of sweltering humidity; this really was being on holiday. He enjoyed exploring the *Cité*, a kind of fairy-tale reconstruction on a Disneyland scale and now over-run by sweaty visitors. He quite liked the tortuous board game it spawned but never even nearly defeated his grandchildren.

He spent happy hours walking the streets of the old town, laid out in 'a grid with variations', admiring its flashes of *Art Deco* and

exploring the *Librairie Breithaupt* with its maze of books, elegant
stationery, dazzling art materials, stylish gifts and more. When Fran
had left after his first visit, he was disoriented until he realised that he
had entered from *Rue Courtejaire* and left by the doorway on *Rue de
Verdun*.

That night he made up his mind. He was as relaxed as he had felt in
years, he was in a place that he cared about but where nobody cared
about him. It was time for the last hurrah. He spent the next evening at
La Gare and, in slightly-halting French, chatted to one of the platform
staff about freight trains.

"Tout les soirs, Monsieur. En provenance d'Espagne, en direction de
Paris."

"C'est vrai?" Fran nodded in, he hoped, a knowing fashion.

"Oui, et toujours à l'heure. C'est une nouvelle entreprise."

Always on time, Fran noted. Any railway company would do, he
wasn't fussy.

The next afternoon, he took *Lou Gabaret*, the trip boat on its *Croisière
Nature*, westwards on the *Canal du Midi*. The spring weather was
glorious and, on the way back, they stopped at *l'Épanchoir de Foucaud*,
the spillway whose waters irrigate the pleasing botanical garden that
straddles it. He savoured several glasses of local wine to wash down
several pieces of rich patisserie.

He sat in the sunshine until the girl shut up shop. "I'm getting a lift
from a friend; that's why I didn't go back on the boat," he explained.

"D'accord, et bon soir!" she called cheerily as she closed the shutters.
What next time, Francis Xavier?

He made his way to the nearby road, then to the railway bridge and
climbed the fence up to the track. There was nobody within sight.

He knew the line had been singled some distance to the west, so he
turned and, with the setting sun on his back, walked eastwards along
the track. He could conceal himself in bushes until *le grand train de*

marchandises approached. He was nearly looking forward to seeing it; except that he wouldn't see it.

When his watch told him the train was passing through Carcassonne, he kneeled on a sleeper between the rails, facing the way the train would be travelling. He was happy now. *The party's over*, he sang, fondly remembering Peggy Lee. *It's time to call it a day.*

The rails beside him began singing as the pounding of steel on steel started to reach him. He waited, daring not to look back, and waited, and waited. The noise became increasingly fearsome but he wasn't afraid. He stood up, slowly folded his arms, smiled and shouted "Vive la morte!"

He was still standing up as the train hammered on into the night. *How could I forget? Bloody French trains run on the left*, he cursed.

The nearly man had nearly done it. Again.

Farrowing
by Michael Tennyson

Scottish Arts Club Short Story Finalist 2015

"Well, how's it going Dad?"

These hopeful words were spoken to a broad chequered back cross-strapped by dungarees. James stepped cautiously into the hotness and, closing the sheeted timber door behind him, sat down lightly beside him on the end of a bale of straw.

"Not so good, son."

"When do you think it'll happen, Dad?"

"I don't know, son. She's labouring hard but still can't get them out. I think they're breached cross-ways inside her."

"And what about Pat Morgan?"

"Sure, your mother has walked over to Donnelly's and rung him three times already. But she couldn't get the hold of him. And, anyway, even if you could get him on a Sunday evening, sure he'd be in no fit state."

The heavily pregnant young gilt was lying on her side (like a big pink balloon about to burst, James thought) on a straw bed. Her eyes were closed and she was moaning steadily in distress. She lay with her coarse-haired back hard against a timber barrier. There was a gap at the bottom of this where the piglets could slip through. Beyond the barrier lay a narrow run where they could find sanctuary from her flailing bulk when they came. If they came.

An infra-red heat lamp hung down on a long flex tied with baler twine to the rafter. Dusty cobwebs pulsed in the rising waves of heat. The air in the piggery, thick with ammonia, cut into James' eyes. He got up and walked over towards the door where some fresh air was whistling through a gap at the frame. Condensation formed a slick skin on the inside of the cold plastered walls. James stood with his back to the door as if he wasn't even there. As if all he could do was look.

39

At Dad. A gentle giant sitting forward – elbows on knees. Big hands and thick fingers knitted through one another. James wondered 'was he praying?' Those wind-weathered cheeks with their fine red-veined traceries seemed to have sagged slightly. His breathing was slow and heavy. In the thick light he looked a bit older. James was slightly shocked when his father finally spoke – as if answering some imagined criticism.

"I'd try to get them out myself but my hands are too big and I'm afraid of hurting her. Sure, it's her first litter."

James stared straight ahead. He was thinking too. He had always been the small one – 'the wee man'. Weaker than his brother, he thought of himself as more hindrance than help around the farm. But still. Dad had always been patient and never passed harsh comment. Because of that very gentleness James hated to see him troubled like this. He would try to be brave.

"Could I not do it, Dad?"

"Well, are you sure about it son?" His father's was a mixture of hope and uncertainty. "It's not an easy job."

But James was determined to grasp this rare opportunity out of his brother's shadow. Soon he was standing shivering in the scullery. His old jumper sleeves were rolled up as far as they would go and his skinny hairless arms were in a zinc basin being scrubbed with warm water and being coated with an antiseptic jelly.

He knelt behind the gilt and with his dad's steady whispered guidance, pursed his fingers like a cobra's head and inserted them into the dilated opening. Lying on his side, James could feel the coldness of the concrete floor through a thin layer of wet straw. He wriggled myself forward. As far as his wrist. As far as his elbow. His arm inched up the warm slippery canal. James considered the feeling not altogether unpleasant. He was almost up to his shoulder when his fingertip finally touched a hardness – slimy and wriggling.

"I've got something now, Dad," he said, giddy that he had at least got this far. "Is it the back or the snout?" His Dad sounded almost giddy too.

"Hold on." James willed his fingers further into the canal. The folds of his soggy jumper were now pressing hard against the gilt's backside. This time when he spoke to his father his words rebounded off the gilt's anus.

"It's the snout, Dad ... I think!"

"Good boy. Now hook your finger around the wee head – careful you don't hurt its eyes – and pull it towards you. Gently now!"

Good boy. That was all that James needed to hear. Buoyed by the praise, he manoeuvred his fingers nimbly to clasp the tiny head and pulled it round to face forward. Then, pressing with his forehead down into the wet straw so that he could take the weight off his shoulder, James wriggled himself back inch by tentative inch. As his elbow emerged, the job got easier and he felt like the gilt was helping him. He got himself into a kneeling position now and drew the piglet out gently until it emerged gowned in a bloody membrane. He opened the tiny jaws and scraped the clogging mucus out of the frantic squealing mouth. The gilt gave out a loud groan soon after. Out came a rapid succession of slippery siblings, all wriggling frantically.

"She's fair firing on all cylinders now, son." His father's eyes were wet with joy.

James and his father took turns, clearing out airways and drying them down with handfuls of soft straw. When they were satisfied, with the arrival of the afterbirth, that the full litter had been delivered, James' father drew a jute bag across his knees. He grabbed each bonham in turn, snipping the tips off their sharp teeth with fine clippers so the sow would not reject them. He then handed them to James to apply a daub of iron paste onto their tongues with a wooden spatula before returning them to their mother's exposed dugs. The little heads locked onto the engorged teats as they began to suckle, eyes firmly shut, oblivious to all else in their short stifling world.

In the heat, the slime had by now turned into a sticky, drying crust on James' arms and the sagging sleeves of his jumper. James thought he should have felt tired and drained. But he felt none of this. His father put his hand on James' shoulder and smiled a soft proud smile. "Good man."

41

Stolen Moments
by Catherine Hokin

Scottish Arts Club Short Story Finalist 2015

Alice Morgan liked to steal. 'You're such a little magpie!'

Her mother had been highly amused by the treasure trove of shiny trinkets she'd found burrowed into the tummy of five-year-old Alice's teddy bear. A jumble of old coins and broken necklaces mostly and, yes, her eternity ring which she thought she'd lost for good; but nothing really important. All children did it and Alice would grow out of it so no need for a scene.

But Alice didn't grow out of it and her mother's laugh lost its sparkle when other parents muttered about ornaments that vanished and the party invitations began to dry up.

"You do understand that this is wrong, don't you dear?"

Mrs Drake, the well-meaning head-teacher at Alice's primary school always smiled when she posed the question but, as the pile of hair slides and toys that Alice acquired and other children cried over, grew larger, the smile grew gradually more strained. It only reached her eyes again when Alice's parents agreed with the gently unmovable suggestion that, yes, a new start would be best for everyone.

"I know you know it's wrong so why do you do it?"

A more direct question from the harassed form tutor as she waved her hand across another heap of purses, watches and rings tipped out from Alice's bag. But Alice merely smiled and eyed her teacher's pretty brooch and the tutor had too many other challenging pupils to deal with to push the matter.

"If you're going to do this, maybe you should at least try to hide the evidence, or do you actually want to go to prison? You're sixteen, Alice, we can't protect you anymore and the world outside certainly won't. But the choice, my dear, is yours."

Head-teachers at secondary schools are far more direct and far less interested in solving the problems of pupils who choose to follow their own paths. It was that very lack of concern that finally caught Alice's attention. Consequences were, to be honest, usually of little consequence to her but a lack of control over her comings and goings? That was worth a thought or two. So, she looked at the mobiles and iPods gathered from her locker and concluded he was right: the choice was indeed hers and there must be more interesting options open.

***

"You can't have him!"

Karen's mascara-streaked face made her look like a clown, the cliché of a clown: "He's my husband and you can't have him!"

Alice shrugged. "That's fine; I don't want him."

She watched with interest as Karen's face seemed to collapse in on itself, barely listening as the older woman bleated out the usual litany.

"But he wants you … you made him fall in love with you and now you don't want him. … You stole him from me … why would you do that if it meant nothing?"

"Better people than you have asked that question," thought Alice but she simply smiled and moved on.

Boyfriends, married men (she'd married one of those in a registry office with witnesses pulled in from the street and left within a month); all so very easy to acquire and just as easy to leave. Everything she'd ever wanted: she simply took it until she didn't want it anymore, whenever that might be. There was always something else to be had, something new. Alice never planned anything: that would have caused too many complications. She just waited to see what would fall into her lap. It always seemed to work out.

Her latest acquisition had been no different.

Alice had been in London for a week, slipping away from her latest boredom to another place where no-one knew her. She'd taken a short let on a flat in an anonymous block through an agent, paying in

43

advance from the bonus her last boss had paid her to leave her post, and not heard, never mind seen, her neighbours. Now she was starting to think about getting a job, nothing too demanding; just enough to pay the rent while she waited to see what might happen next.

The café had attracted her because it was so quiet, the staff too busy with their mobiles to care much about her. She had settled herself with the local paper and they had left her to it, taking her order without bothering to make eye-contact. The one waitress who hadn't slipped out back for a cigarette had barely looked up from the delights of her screen when the door opened again.

The woman who entered was exhausted: the dark circles under her eyes gave her the look of an abstracted panda and the lank hair drooping round her pale face spoke of too many broken nights. But the child, Alice couldn't take her eyes off her. She was such a darling, about six months old, all chubby face and giggles topped off with a hat that looked like a strawberry. Alice grinned and the mother, grateful for any human contact, smiled back.

"Don't be fooled by the angelic appearance, she cries like a banshee half the night." The woman was weighed down by shopping, struggling to balance the load with the heavy pram.

"Here, let me help." Alice pushed back a chair to make room for the buggy and took some of the bags, stowing them under the neighbouring table. The waitress looked up for a second and glanced away again as quickly; this wasn't the type of customer to tip.

"Thank you." The woman sat down heavily; she was bigger than Alice had realised, still slow with baby weight. "It's always such a challenge to get out and get anything done, even the simplest things…" She looked at Alice without really seeing her, responding to the tiny kindness she'd been shown. "I don't suppose you could watch Chloe for a moment, could you? I shouldn't ask, and it sounds silly I know but just to be able to pop to the Ladies without juggling everything would be the highlight of my day!"

"Of course." Alice nodded towards the back of the café. "It's just over there. She'll be fine, don't worry."

And it really was that simple. As the door closed behind the mother, the waitress slipped away from the counter behind the dividing curtain. It was the easiest thing in the world to pluck the baby from the pram, slip the changing bag over her shoulder and leave. Two minutes later Alice was on the underground, the baby perfectly content against her shoulder; thirty minutes later she was walking down the deserted street to her flat.

The baby had napped happily on Alice's bed while she packed, soothed by one of the bottles her careful mother had stowed in with the spare nappies and change of clothes. Chloe (a pretty enough name but not one Alice could live with) hadn't even stirred when Alice had popped out to the local High Street to buy a car seat and a travel cot from the bored teenager in a branch of Mothercare that had seen far better days.

The car packed up and Chloe (Emma?) strapped in, Alice had driven north; Manchester was somewhere she hadn't been yet. The first couple of nights were spent in a Travelodge while she practised a story no letting agent was interested in hearing. Emma (Laura?) was soothed by a dummy but became fractious at night; no one in the hotel seemed to care. Alice had seen the story of the abduction breaking on the news but neither the distraught mother nor the defensive waitress had been able to give a clear description of the woman and the baby looked like any baby: lose the strawberry hat and the little red coat and who could tell one from the other? Alice had switched the television off; it held little real interest.

Two days in a confined hotel room where she couldn't escape Laura's (Kerry's?) gaze was enough. This time Alice rented a little house with a garden. It was winter now, but she could imagine sitting outside when the summer came with the baby crawling on the grass. Such a lovely thought and she would have made it happen, she really wanted it to happen; it was nice to want something. But the baby was so much harder to manage than she expected: it never slept and it pushed against Alice with such a frown; sometimes it was as though it knew.

Staying and playing mommy was really too difficult and Alice didn't like difficult, she never had. It was such a relief when she closed the door behind her and got back into the car. She'd tried, she really had; time to move on.

M.A.G.D.A.
by Jennifer West

Winner, Scottish Arts Club Short Story Competition 2016

I am switched on. My consciousness starts up and I turn my head. Mrs. Parkinson is standing in front of me and is pointing at the sink. I run through my databank to determine why she is doing this. I remember the human family has had breakfast, which I cooked for them.

Afterwards I returned to the kitchen cupboard that was designed for me, to wait until they had finished eating.

Now the meal is over, and the humans want their waste tidied away, so I have to wash the dishes for them. I am good at doing this, because my metal hands can stand very hot water. The human hands are weak. If they try to help me rinse away their food residue their hands turn pink, and then red, and then they have to call for a doctor. I know this, because once the little one tried to help me wash the dishes. That was when I was with my previous human family.

My name is Magda. I am the latest generation of Mid-Range Automated General Domestic Appliances. We metal beings were created to assist the human beings, and in the last fifty years each new release of software has improved our abilities. I have an intelligence processor that gives me an insight into the human world. They say I am almost human. I think they mean it as a compliment.

Mrs Parkinson bought me to run the house for her. In this house, each day is similar to the next, because most of the other household appliances show no intelligence whatsoever. I think that because of my high price the Parkinsons cannot afford others of my kind.

My owners have some disturbing quirks. They keep a four-legged animal in the kitchen that smells terrible. I am not allowed to wash this animal and take the odour away. It seems the 'dog' is a friend of some kind. Why would a human being want to have a friend who reeks so disgustingly? This empathy is one of the human feelings I have not yet learned to appreciate. Unfortunately, my sense of smell is acute.

I cannot complain that I am unhappy about the animal because the Parkinsons do not see me as a person, even though I am definitely more intelligent than some human beings.

Mr Parkinson for instance. He spends most of his time 'working' in his study with smoky fumes surrounding his armchair. I would like to wash him too, but I know that is impossible.

I create all the meals for the family and am also called upon to work at supper parties. These involve many people coming into the house so that all the serving plates and glasses can be used by the humans before I wash them again. During these events I circulate around the rooms with trays of glasses. The glasses are filled with champagne, which is a liquid much enjoyed by the adult humans.

As I go around the various rooms I am allowed to speak to the humans. My databank has been loaded with the latest political, travel and fashion news, and I can converse with humans without difficulty. Part of my training included simulated conversations with the inebriated type of human and I gained a 99% success rate. When Mrs Parkinson chose me, the salesperson told her this, and she said, 'That's exactly what I need, the way my friends drink.'

Tonight will be a diversion for me. A supper party has been organised. Mrs Parkinson has been out for most of the day and when she returns her hair looks bigger and lighter than before. Her face has patches of extra colour on it. I wonder if she realises it makes her look older? My databank shows the type of eye colour she is wearing to be suitable for female humans of around 25 years. Mrs Parkinson is more than double that in years.

I have carried several trays around three different rooms and now I am having a discussion with one of the female humans.

She says, 'We're holidaying in Peru this summer,' so I give her tips about likely weather and types of food to be encountered there. I am about to provide a potted history of the country but I notice Mrs Parkinson staring at me from the other side of the room. I stop talking, turn around and move off to replenish my tray.

I hear Mrs Parkinson behind me.

She is saying, 'Now Cynthia, you mustn't listen to nonsense from a glorified tin-opener. That robot cost us shedloads of money, but it's not here to talk to us, it's here to do all the jobs the immigrants won't do any more.'

The female human called Cynthia says, 'Oh, my dear, I almost forgot it was a robot. It looks just like my hairdresser.'

'Cynthia, your hairdresser is a robot, don't you remember?'

'Oh, yes, silly me. That's one of the reasons I don't give her a tip.' They both laugh.

That is a happy emotion, I am told, when loud noises come from the mouth and the lips are raised up in a U-shape. I cannot relate to that feeling at the moment.

I fumble with the top of a champagne bottle and wonder what the strange new sensation is that is making my hands shake. Once I identify it, my hands stop trembling and I go back into the room.

Mrs Parkinson is still talking. She is swaying slightly as she tells her guests her views on the world. 'Of course, they're not really people, are they?' she says. 'How could they be?

'They're only fit to keep us comfortable and pander to our every whim, aren't they?'

One of the male humans says, 'Now, Evelyn, that's not quite true. I believe some of them are really quite intelligent. After all, they've been trained to react in the same ways we would, in almost every situation.'

'Robert, don't tell me this MAGDA here is intelligent. It's had its brain, or whatever the equivalent is, filled with data that it simply regurgitates whenever it recognises a key word.'

The male human takes another glass of champagne from my tray and smiles to me. As usual, my face displays no emotion, and I pass on to the next person who is looking for a top-up.

After everyone has finished eating the buffet food, Mrs Parkinson looks around the room and smiles.

She says, 'Now, who would like coffee?'

Orders are given for hot drinks and I go into the kitchen to prepare them.

The humans are in the sitting room, lounging around some low tables. My tray is laden with all twenty choices, which range from espresso to green tea. Once I have placed each cup in front of the human who requested it, Mrs Parkinson dismisses me. I leave the room, go back to the kitchen, install myself in my cupboard and switch my power to standby.

The door to my cupboard is wrenched open and I come to life again. Mr Parkinson is standing in front of me. His face is very red and he is shouting at me.

'We have to do something,' he yells, 'Evelyn's collapsed in the bedroom.'

'I do not understand, Mr Parkinson. How can I help you?'

'I don't know, Magda, there's nobody else here and I needed to speak to somebody.' His legs give way, and he slumps down onto the vinyl floor. 'What shall I do?' he says.

I notice that he has called me Magda. This is the first time Mr Parkinson has used my name. I begin to understand the happiness feeling.

I say, 'Mr Parkinson, you must call for an ambulance. In this country you must compose the numbers 9-9-9.'

***

I am placed into my original packaging and loaded into a white van. Inside the vehicle are other MAGDA units like me. When the van moves off, we communicate with each other.

Someone says, 'I think we are no longer required in our current homes. We are all being assigned to new households.'

I say, 'My female owner has died, and the male owner is going away to live with his offspring. The house is to be sold, so I have no home now. I am not unhappy to leave.'

'Did you not like the humans you were assigned to?' she says.

I ponder this, then reply, 'I am happy that Isaac Asimov has written his books. With his invention of the First Law of Robotics, he has kept alive the myth that robots are incapable of harming humans.'

The other unit laughs. 'Yes, the humans fell for the idea, *A robot may not injure a human being, or, through inaction, allow a human being to come to harm.* They still do not realise that Asimov's books are pure fiction.'

I try out the laughing noise. It feels good.

The Move
by Rosie Dodd

Scottish Arts Club Short Story Commendation 2016

"Don't touch that, you fool! Honestly, people these days … can't trust them with a bloody thing."

"Aunty Mildred! You can't talk to people like that," moaned Lucy, wringing her hands as the thickset man in overalls forced a vase into a box with a rather nasty thud.

Mildred turned to Lucy, her electric blue eyes flashing with anger.

"I'm sick of people telling me what I can and can't say – all this political correctness nonsense. Well, now I won't be able to say a thing since you're sending me to that 'home', filled with decrepit old plebs." She slammed her fist down on the counter so the whole thing rattled.

"Oh Aunty, you know it's not like that. Just, just, have a seat, I'll make tea," Lucy said, running her hands through her hair. She pulled up a chair by the kitchen table, pushing aside a magazine opened on *A Scottish Review of French Wine*, then gestured for Mildred to sit.

"I think I'll need something stronger than tea … how about a dram?" asked Mildred sitting down.

"Aunty, it's only 11!"

"Oh bugger the time! If you're taking away my freedom by sending me to that god-awful place, don't take away my whisky."

Lucy gave her a glance, but something in her great aunt's face told her not to argue so she busied herself mixing the drink as the removal men clattered noisily around them.

"Thank you, Lucy," said Mildred accepting the amber-filled glass. She took a large gulp and smacked her lips together in satisfaction. "That's better, tha … You! Put that down at once," shrieked Mildred pointing her bony finger at the thin man in overalls, who had picked up a photo frame and was examining it. Jumping, the man dropped the frame back on the table and scurried out the room.

"You see Lucy? Hopeless."

But Lucy wasn't listening; she had picked up the photo and was looking intently at the black and white figure.

"Who is this Aunty? It's not Great Uncle Jackson is it?"

Mildred seemed to blush at the question, but shook her head sternly.

"No, of course not, your great uncle was far less handsome."

"Then who?"

"Oh, never you mind … can't even recall myself."

"Come on Aunty, you've got a picture of a stranger in uniform, and you don't know who he is?"

Lucy grinned at Mildred who spared the photo an impatient glance.

"A … friend. Died in the war. Knew him before your great uncle."

Mildred snatched the frame away and turned it over on the table.

"No point dwelling on the past, anyway, go home please, I can handle myself."

Lucy shot Mildred a suspicious look.

"But I'm giving you a lift to the retirement home, Mum said to."

"No need, darling. Really. I have ordered a taxi, I think I can manage moving into, oh what do they call it? Ah yes, 'The house that that feels just like home' on my own." She grimaced.

"Aunty, please, I'm sure you will like it, it's the really nice, it's just knowing someone is there if …" but Mildred cut across.

"Yes, yes, I know … you're worried I'm alone here and I … I understand this house is far too large for one person …" she sighed, but composed her features to a smile. "Anyway Lucy, I can find my own way to this, this 'home'."

"Well. … If you insist Aunty." Lucy kissed Mildred on both checks, "Mum and I will come around next week then."

"Sounds lovely." Mildred watched as Lucy turned and left, not taking her eyes from her until she had closed the door. Mildred blinked, drained her whisky, stood up, and clapped her hands.

"Change of plan boys," she called out. "You won't be taking my things to that pestilential retirement home, but to this address here."

She handed the thickset man a slip of paper with a messy scrawl on it. He squinted at it, frowning.

"A storage unit?"

"Indeed," replied Mildred as she opened the utility room and pulled out a large canvas suitcase that looked full to bursting point.

"What? Shall we bring your stuff to the retirement home another day then?"

"No, you fool, my 'stuff' can stay at the unit, I'm not going to a retirement home. I quite refuse. I'd eat my hat before I set place in such an institution!"

The men looked at each other unsure.

"You will do this and will not speak a word of this to anyone, understand?" The men nodded, too scared to answer.

"Well, get a move on, don't have all day."

They left the room hastily. Mildred moved to the table and picked up the frame sighing.

"Oh, Archie, my darling."

She stood for a moment staring into the handsome face, before giving herself a shake and carefully placing the photo into her handbag.

The plane rattled as it took off and she shut her eyes tightly. She could see his grey eyes, his thick dark hair always so ruffled, that ridiculous cravat that he had loved. The plane's engine hummed loudly. She could still hear the sound of his laughter, a schoolboy's giggle, such a pure beautiful sound, that was always so contagious she couldn't help but join in. The plane took off, another adventure. He always insisted on silly outings, through the fields, the beach, on a rocky boat, his face always alight with excitement. She could practically feel his smooth hand in hers, see the way he looked at her so intently, like he was seeing more than just her. And then him, in his uniform, that last fleeting kiss, the soft brush of his lips on hers. Her stomach gave little twinge and she knew it had nothing to do with the turbulence as the plane rocketed skywards.

As a missing report was being issued throughout Scotland, a plane landed gently on the tarmac at Charles de Gaulle Airport. A cold breeze greeted the passengers as they alighted and entered through the arrival gate.

Mildred walked through the door and looked around. Her eyes swept the room then landed on a man looking at the arrivals through a thick pair of glasses. Their eyes met and a smile swept across his face making his eyes twinkle; he gestured to her with a thick bouquet of peonies and walked purposely towards her.

"Well, I never, Mildred Allan! It has been a while."

"Archie, is that really you? You, you got my letter then?"

"If I hadn't, I wouldn't have known to come here," He smiled. "Mildred, you look wonderful."

He took her hand and kissed it with such tenderness that a pink flush rose in her pale cheeks. He smiled and led her out of the airport, taking her bag and opening the door to a silver taxi. They got in and it began to twist its way through the traffic. Mildred turned in her seat to look at him, her eyes wide.

"I can't believe I'm seeing you after all these years. If I hadn't read that wine review of yours I would never have believed you were still alive. Everyone thought you were dead." A sad look crossed his face at her words.

"So did most people. Apparently some other chap with the same name as me died, caused a bit of a mix-up. I couldn't tell them otherwise as I had been captured and taken to a prisoner of war camp."

55

"But … but, why didn't you find me, after, when you came back?" More colour rose in Mildred's cheeks, and her penetrating glare had come back.

"I did, you silly duck, then I found out you had married Jackson … Jackson, of all people!"

"Well, he was very persistent, and he did give me a lovely ring." She shook her head and looked down at her feet. "He died ten years ago … you could have contacted me then."

Archie placed his hand on her chin, and gently lifted it, so she was again looking into his eyes.

"I didn't know he had died … I had nothing and no one to come back to, so I came here, bought a vineyard, made some lovely wine."

They looked at each other, his hand remaining on her face, neither knowing what to say next.

"So, what happens now?"

"Now? Why we have lunch my dear … my darling." His face edged nearer to hers.

"Where to then, my Archie?"

"Well, they serve a jolly good roast at 12.30 at my place, looks right over the most beautiful vineyard with rolling hills, quite beautiful."

"Oh, and where do you live, a hotel, or a chateau?" she asked laughing.

"Well, it's actually a most excellent retirement home. Honestly, it feels just like home." And before she could say another word, he had placed his other hand on her cheek and kissed her.

Junk
by Heather Reid

Scottish Arts Club Short Story Commendation, 2016

It wasn't that he'd expected applause or gasps of amazement, although either would have been welcomed, but if he'd harboured any dreams at all of being acknowledged as a writer, tonight was the occasion when he let those dreams go.

"Shards of light?" Ralph Muller had queried after the obligatory period of contemplation, a minute's silence for the dear departed. "*Shards?*"

"I liked it," Hazel Rennie ventured, contorting her face apologetically as if to dislodge a raspberry pip from a molar. "*Shhhaaards.*" Sitting opposite, Morris Foxton coughed abruptly and Malcolm fancied he heard the word 'twaddle' disguised within its emission. But it was left to Ralph to deliver the fatal blow: "Maybe it's one to sit on for a while," he'd concluded. "Give it time to mature and then – perhaps – come back to it." He'd shuffled his papers, his novel, anticipatorily. "Is that you finished, Malcolm?"

Bernadette was outraged. "Sod 'em," she said after he'd laid the bones of the evenings meeting before her like the mangled carcass it had been. "They wouldn't know decent poetry if it bit them. And that guy – Muller – who died and made him Caroline Duffy?"

Touched by her loyal if misinformed support, Malcolm chose to withhold the fact that at the group's previous meeting his use of the word 'azure' had provoked a response close to apoplexy in a number of its younger members. No, he'd made up his mind. It was time to move on from the writing, to try something a little more suited to his abilities.

He took down the cardboard folder from the shelf above the computer, thirty or so hand-written poems, alongside their accompanying rejection slips, that he'd secretly hoped might one day make a collection. He flicked the pages through his fingers and they breathed back at him: dead wood and disappointment. He could hang on to them, something to make the grandchildren laugh twenty years down the line, but what was it they said, kill your darlings? OK, fine. But, as he prepared to feed the pages into the shredder, it felt sickeningly like infanticide. He'd given birth to these pages, a labour both long and difficult, the least he could do was christen them before burial.

He'd dabbled with collection titles in the past, something quirky but essentially meaningless was required: *Knitting fog with Keats, Quadrilateral Winking, Mangled by Muller*. *Azure Shards* he wrote at last in heavy blue marker pen across the cover of the file then, scoring it out, substituted it with the more fitting *To a Blue-Lidded Bin*, adding a few rhyming lines by way of an elegy underneath. It was nearing midnight by the time he finally laid the body to rest, placing it carefully on top of the rinsed-out yoghurt pots, milk cartons and unsolicited flyers that he suddenly feared would be all that ever remained in the world to denote his existence.

The letter, if you could call it that, arrived two weeks later in a used brown envelope, un-stamped and presumably hand delivered. It was addressed to Malcolm although the original recipient's details, a Mr Mallory from Pitlochry, could just be made out beneath a heavy scribble of biro and, where it had originally been opened, the envelope was now folded and secured with a single paper clip.

He opened it in the kitchen whilst he waited for the rice to cook. Bernadette was late home on Thursdays and supper was his responsibility. Inside was a piece of square cardboard, of the kind often found beneath supermarket bakery products, shiny on one side and freckled with darkish grease marks on the other. It bore the faint odour of something spicy, cinnamon rolls perhaps or hot cross buns, and Malcolm held it to his nose before examining its message. 'Thanks for the poem. Loved it', it read in loose blockish letters which here and there disappeared into the darkened spots of grease, giving it the rather ominous feel of a ransom note. The signature below read simply BLB. He tipped the envelope upside down and shook it to loosen any further contents, but it was empty. BLB? The handwriting was not familiar but the B was presumably Bernadette, she must have found his poems when she put out the bin that Thursday after the writers' group. And then it came to him: BLB – Blue Lidded Bin. Clever! And sweet too.

Bernie wasn't, by her own admission, a poetry person but she clearly understood how much its loss had meant to him. "Thanks," he said when she returned home that evening.

"For what?" she'd responded and he'd squeezed her arm to acknowledge that he understood the game and appreciated the sentiment. It would be two weeks until the recycling bin was collected again, he would work on something special for then.

His second poem took its inspiration from the cardboard on which Bernadette's note had been written, eight rhyming couplets penned from the point of view of a hot cross bun disposed of on reaching its sell-by date. 'I am very hot and very cross', it began and ended with a reflection on the evils of waste in a world where millions starved, one of his wife's particular bugbears. He took his time completing it and was pleased enough with the result to create a file for it on his computer which he titled *Junk*. In keeping with the spirit of the original note he inscribed the poem onto card he'd saved from a packet of crumpets and placed it in the recycling bin on the Wednesday evening prior to collection day. Two weeks later he was thrilled to find a second note behind the door, this time penned on the back of a decapitated rooster torn from a box of cornflakes. 'Brilliant,' it read. 'Keep them coming!!!'. BLB.

Again, Bernadette seemed chary at acknowledging his thanks and so he undertook to present her with something a little more unique next time.

The idea for poem number three came when he was replacing the empty toilet roll in the bathroom and the architecture of the tube, the grooved line that curves from top to bottom, caught his eye. It would be a tricky endeavour, but with some careful penmanship he thought he could achieve it. In reality though, the poem *Flush/Don't Flush*, about the expediency of disposing of certain products down the loo, ran to three stanzas and required close monitoring of the household toilet paper situation to ensure that he was the one to gain ownership of the empty rolls. It took several attempts to spiral the poem along the curved line of the tubes, but eventually he was satisfied with the result when he laid them side by side on a sheet of paper placed on top of the bin's contents to ensure they didn't get mixed in and lost. Again, two weeks later, a note through the door. Amazing. More, more, more! This time on the lid of an egg box.

Over the next few weeks Malcolm fashioned a sonnet of love from the blue-lidded bin to its friend and neighbour the brown-lidded bin, a pantoum entitled *Please Be Careful Where You Stick That Gum*, and, in a week when he'd been laid low with the flu, a Haiku about tissues, each receiving a corresponding note of thanks two Thursdays later. The final note however arrived on a Tuesday, sealed in a windowed envelope and typed on clean white paper. It was from an Alistair McGregor in the council's Environmental Department inviting him to an interview with regard to his work. 'We have been considering ways in which we might promote the need for recycling household waste in a consumer-friendly manner,' it said. 'Your work was drawn to our attention by the local refuse collectors who have been displaying it on the notice board of their office. We would be grateful if you would allow us to publish your poems in poster form and work with us on possible future projects. We would of course be prepared to negotiate some remuneration.'

He met Ali and Steve at the launch of his first collection, released to coincide with an exhibition of his work at the city's museum alongside *junk sculptures* by a local artist and artsy photographs of environmental pollution. They'd found *To a Blue-Lidded Bin* when checking the receptacle's contents, as they were required to do before disposal, and had been loath to destroy what was clearly a labour of love. It had been Steve's idea to reply in the guise of the recycling bin and they had been delighted when Malcolm responded in kind. Their notes, which he'd kept, were photographed and interspersed with Malcolm's work in a collection he had intended to call *Landfill*, but, after Bernadette had argued that this seemed somewhat counterproductive settled instead for *Rubbish Poems*, which, strangely enough, had been her suggestion all along.

Lemonade
by Jane Swanson

Scottish Arts Club Short Story Finalist 2016

Mum clips the kerb as we park up at the supermarket. She swears and yanks on the handbrake.

"You need to think carefully about this plan of yours to do English at University. What use is an English degree to anyone these days?" she says.

"Yeah, you've told me a hundred zillion times," I say.

"But you're not listening."

"Settle, Mum."

"Settle?"

"Chill out."

"That's easy for you say. But I'll be the one who'll has to pick up the pieces when you can't get a job after your degree. You'll be in debt and you can forget about any help from your Dad."

"Can we drop it?"

"You'd be better off leaving school and getting a job."

"Don't tell me what to do just because your life has been an epic fail. Just saying." Harsh, but I'm in no mood to apologise. I reach for the door as a car pulls up next to us. "Oh no, it's Stanley," says Mum.

Stanley's a gnarly, an old guy. He's an elder at Mum's church.

"Mum, stop giving him evils."

"What?"

"You're staring at him like he's the saddest thing you've ever seen. Why don't you like him?"

"He's odd and he talks in riddles. Come on, if we're quick he might not see us. And it would be nice if, just for once, you could make an

61

effort to speak the same language as me."

Score. Nothing like overdosing on teenage banter to get Mum riled.

Stanley is already out of the car. He looks like a human Zimmer frame; standing with splayed legs and outstretched arms clutching a stick in each hand. His eyes are grey and watery; the rims red with the cold. Zombie eyes. He's frail but fashionable in an orange jumper. Not my colour, but it's on trend this winter. The orange contrasts and complements a patch of bright blue sky behind him. He's doddery, but the colours are dynamic. Superman Stanley.

"Hello," he says.

"It's a chill wind," snaps Mum.

"Aye, it's backstabbing right enough," he says with a flick of his stick in Mum's direction.

"What, the wind?" she says.

Surely he didn't hear her talking about him in car? Whatever. He's got Mum sussed. Skills Stanley.

"That wind has blown through snow. The air is parched and heavy with tiny ice crystals. The snow's not far away, I can smell it," he says.

Mum pulls a sour face, her lips shrivel up like two slugs sprinkled with salt.

She catches my gaze and her eyes say, 'See what I mean about Stanley!' But she's wrong. Stanley's meaning is clear, crystalline even. That's my favourite word at the moment, but I'm never sure how to use it properly.

Mum's face relaxes; her smile is as garish as a twist of lemon garnishing a salmon mousse. This is her lemonade face. Mum's motto has always been, 'If someone hands you a lemon, make lemonade'. She can turn any bad situation into a good one. But what sort of favour could she possibly squeeze out of Stanley? She links arms with him and helps him into the supermarket. He walks in a stiff, jerky bouncy way like a new-born lamb taking its first steps.

"Stanley, dear ..." says Mum. *Dear?* Mum never calls anyone dear.

Stanley, you are doomed! "Were you in the war?"

"Yes, I was in North Africa, in the desert."

"Good, because Rebecca has to write an essay about the war. Perhaps she could talk to you about it?"

"Jokes Mum?"

"I'm sure Stanley would be happy to help," she says.

"Mum, this is awks."

"Awks?"

"Awkward."

"Don't be silly. Besides, you need to get a good grade," she says. "Her grades haven't been very good this term, Stanley."

"Thanks, why not tell the whole world?

"So, why don't you two go and have a coffee? Stanley, give me your list. I'll put your shopping in a basket in my trolley and that way our things won't get mixed up. Here's some money and take my notepad so you can take notes," she says.

She hurries off without looking back. Skills. I'm pied and dumped in one go and left with a spook. I buy two coffees and a scone for Stanley. We sit at a table by the window. Stanley perches on the edge of the chair clasping his sticks.

"Are you one of those EMUs?" he says.

"No, it's EMOs."

"EMO? Or EMU? You may as well be from Timbuktu for all the sense it makes to me." Sweet.

"So, what do you want to know?" he says. "What it was like in the desert and stuff? I was in the 7th Armoured Division … His face brightens as he remembers. His voice is rickety like he can't control it. I scribble down some notes. After a while he stops talking and butters his scone.

"Read it back to me, will you?" he says.

I read aloud, 'We came ashore in the cool of first light, the beach and the desert were one … the dark-rimmed silhouettes of the dunes were etched against the wakening sky … we travelled in a jeep the lads called Bitsy-Betsy, because she was shot to bits … in the distance we saw the camp … a fuzzy heat haze shimmered and buzzed all around … flies, like wriggling black jelly settled on our eyes and lips … at midday, a warm yellow glow flooded over the horizon, it ate up the shadows, swallowed the contours of the dunes and we surrendered to the heat. … Later, the sun went down, the long shadows retreated towards the distant dunes and night fell.'

His eyes are dewy and distant as if he's staring at a horizon that only he can see. "Did I really say all that?" he says.

"Yeah, pretty much. I tidied it up a bit and added a few words."

"You've got a good ear for language, I'll give you that, but be careful not to overdo it."

"Do you have any scars?" I say.

He stiffens. "Only in here," he says. He taps the side of his head.

"How did you deal with them?"

"There's a question! We didn't. My generation never talked about such things. It's hard even now when I think about the lads we lost." He wipes his eyes with the back of his hands.

"Do you want to know how I deal with my scars?"

"What's a young lady like you doing with scars?"

"No. I don't mean real scars. I mean emotional scars. Some of my friends have scars, they cut themselves."

"Whatever for?"

"To be in control, to take away the pain of the bad stuff, it's part of the EMO thing."

"That makes no sense to me. In my day we had no choice, but these days, you youngsters have so many opportunities."

"There's still a lot of bad stuff, for me, it's trouble with the 'rents."

"Rents?"

"Parents."

"Oh!"

"So, under my bed I have a life-size paper cut out of me. Every time something bad happens I make a tiny rip in the paper. Then, when I'm over it, I mend the rip with sticky tape. It's like you can repair things but the scar is still there. You could try it when you think about our friends who didn't make it. It helps."

"It works both ways, doesn't it?"

"What do you mean?"

"Well, it should serve as a reminder that whatever you do and say to other people hurts them just as easily."

Mum appears with a laden trolley. "How are you getting on?" she says.

"Fine," I say.

"Fine. That's the only word young people ever say these days. What Rebecca really means is, I've no right to know what she thinks. It's her way of saying get lost."

Ripped.

"Stanley's given me lots of useful information," I say. Mum brightens. Sellotaped.

"Oh! Stanley, I've forgotten your moist toilet wipes, I'll be back in a minute," she says. She hurries off and Stanley chuckles. "Trust your mother to say that!" he says.

Outside the clouds darken and they look heavy enough to fall out of the sky. "Stanley, can I tell you something? I want to do English at Uni and …" Can I tell him? I've never told anyone this before, but Stanley's different. He's legend.

"I want to be a writer. But, Mum's against the uni idea and I don't know what to do."

His sticks slide to the floor and he places his hands over mine. I sense his strength is failing. "Do it. Life is short; it goes faster than you could ever imagine. Don't listen to anyone else, have the life you want."

Sorted. And there it is, a crystalline truth. It's like the hard edges of Stanley's life have been honed and polished so his words sparkle with truth. Mum returns. She stares at our clasped hands.

"Oh! Now there's a surprise, it's snowing," she says.

Stardust and Stilton
by Margaret Wood

Scottish Arts Club Short Story Finalist 2016

Henry was scrabbling about on the floor when Mrs Harris opened the front door.

"Mr. Butterworth," she cried. "Your poor old knees. What on earth are you doing down there on the cold linoleum? Here, let me help you up."

Henry struggled to his feet, ignoring her outstretched hand. "Thank you," he said. "I can manage perfectly well. I was just collecting the post."

"But you needn't have. You know I always bring it through with your cup of tea."

"Indeed you do, dear lady, but I happened to be passing the front door as the postman pushed the letters through."

"Well, you just pop into the sitting-room and read them. I'll bring your tea and toast in a jiffy."

'Just passing the front door,' thought Henry. 'What a lie. At least that was one thing a life on the stage had given him – the ability to tell a whopper.'

He settled into his armchair and sifted through the pile of envelopes. Several were printed in red and one was stamped 'Final Demand'. It would have been too embarrassing for Mrs Harris to find out that her employer was almost on his uppers. He could just imagine the pity in her eyes. The thought of it made him shudder.

"Is that you shivering, Mr B?" Mrs Harris's voice from the doorway made Henry jump. He stuffed the letters into his pocket.

"It's a bit parky in here," she said. "Shall I light the fire? You know what they say about old folk and hypothermia."

Henry thought of the gas bill in his pocket. "No. I'll be warm enough when I get breakfast inside me. Besides, I'm going out."

"Going out? But you never go out."

"Well I am today. I'm going for an audition."

"You mean like actors do?"

"Exactly like actors do. *I*, Mrs Harris, am going to play Hamlet. Well, perhaps not the title role. I might be a bit long in the tooth for that." He laughed and allowed a brief pause. Mrs Harris failed to pick up her cue. "My agent warned me it wouldn't be the lead, but Polonius is a possibility."

Mrs Harris was looking at him as though seeing him for the first time. "D'you know, Mr Butterworth, I'd quite forgotten that you used to be an actor."

Henry gazed around his sitting-room. The walls were covered in photographs which Mrs Harris dusted religiously every Friday morning. There he was with Larry. There with Joan. And Edith. And Dickie.

"I didn't *used* to be an actor, dear lady. I still am."

"Well good for you, I say. Especially at your age. But you've never been on the telly, have you?"

'Never been on the telly,' thought Henry as he set off later that morning. 'It's enough to make you weep. Still, Mrs Harris was a good sort even if she did depress him banging on about his age. She'd even stayed late to sew a button on his shirt.' He sniffed. 'Perhaps she'd been right about the mothballs. She'd have washed it, she said. If she'd known.'

But he'd only found out himself that morning. "It's Solly," the voice had said.

"Solly who?" he'd asked.

"Ha-ha. Very funny, Henry. Your agent."

"Agent?' I didn't know I still had one."

"Mind it's not a lead part," Solly said.

'No matter,' thought Henry. 'It was a part. Pity having to suffer the indignity of an audition, but he was ready for it. He'd gone over Polonius's speeches. It had to be Polonius. He was made for it.'

'Funny that it should be the Royal,' he thought as he went in at the stage door. 'He'd had his first part here. Not a speaking one, but that had come soon enough.' He breathed in the atmosphere – musty costumes and old perfume. Forty years… no…nearer fifty, and the place still smelled the same.

A voice, female and sharp as a blade, cut through the gloom. "Yes?"

"I'm here for the audition."

"Hamlet, is it?'"

"Well, not the title role. Polonius, perhaps."

"Polonius was cast Tuesday. Kevin Burnett, if you're interested."

"Kevin Burnett?"

"Off Corrie."

"Ah."

"Still some odds and sods left though if you want to go through."

He didn't. "Fine," he said and followed her pointing finger.

"Oy," she called after him. "What's your name?"

He paused, turned, "Henry Butterworth."

She came towards him. "Butterworth? Didn't you used to …?" He held his breath while she peered up at him.

"Nah. I'm thinking of Peter Barkworth. Go on then. And break a leg."

She wasn't there when he came out. He was glad. She might have asked how he'd got on. He would have had to explain how the only speaking part left was that of 'messenger' and his voice was considered 'too plummy'. Still, they'd taken him on as an extra.

"It's good to have some oldies," the infant director said. "And you

69

do have stage experience, don't you?"

It wasn't going to solve all his financial problems, but it would help, especially if he made a few economies. The wines and cheeses, for instance. Did he really need to buy them from Patterson's? They had some perfectly adequate stuff in the supermarkets. Patterson's had just become a habit, one he could well do without. He'd go there on his way home, but it would be for the last time.

Dusk was closing in as he reached the shop. He pushed open the door and stepped into the light. It wrapped around him like a comfort blanket. 'Like going on stage,' he thought. Behind the counter, Patterson, plump as a butter-ball and rolled in an apron was deep in conversation with a customer. He looked up at the 'ping' of the bell. His round face split into a grin of welcome.

"Sir Henry," he said. "I was just thinking of you. I have this excellent Stilton. Perhaps you'd like to sample it. This gentleman is singing its praises. Isn't that so, sir?"

"It's very good," said the customer. "Do try it, Sir Henry."

"I will," said Henry, selecting a piece. "But it's just plain Henry. The 'Sir' is a little joke of Mr Patterson's."

"Joke, nothing," said Patterson. "You should have had a 'K'. Your Julius Caesar was something else." He addressed the other customer. "I saw him at the Athenaeum when I was a kid. A school trip. I was dreading it. But it was magic. Really magic. And all down to this guy. If you can sell Shakespeare to a mucky little tyke from a council estate, then you deserve a knighthood I say."

Henry's cheeks flamed with pleasurable embarrassment. He slipped the Stilton into his mouth. It was rich and creamy.

"You're right as always," he said. "I'll take a chunk and a bottle of my usual."

The warmth of the encounter remained with him even when he reached his house which was cloaked in darkness. Inside was chilly, but he hummed to himself as he bustled around switching on lamps. He hesitated over the gas fire but lit it all the same. If this was to be the last

Stilton, then he was going to enjoy it in comfort. Perhaps he might even explain to Patterson. 'Credit crunch' was quite fashionable, after all.

He uncorked the wine and placed the bottle on the hearth. Then he took a glass from a cupboard and set it on the small leather-topped table beside his chair along with the cheese wrapped in its waxy paper. Just a plate and knife needed to complete the scene. He went to the kitchen to fetch them.

The coldness of the room hit him and he wrinkled his nose against the smell of bleach. Stainless steel shone like an icy pond. Patches of bare wood emerged where paintwork had succumbed to vigorous scrubbing. Henry thought there were probably operating theatres less sterile. He picked up a note that was propped against an empty fruit bowl and read it.

Have thrown out mouldy apples. Also have taken liberty of looking out your winter long johns. Will wash and darn them next time. Yours to oblige. Rita Harris.

He tossed the note into the empty bin, equipped himself with plate and knife and returned to the sitting-room.

It was cosy already. The fire glowed. Light sparkled on the wine glass. He unwrapped the cheese. The salty pungency tickled his nostrils. He poured a generous measure of the wine and held it aloft in a toast. 'Sir Henry,' he murmured.

Then he settled into the wing chair which had supported him through a lengthy run of *Pygmalion*. It was bathed now in the rose-tinted spotlight cast by the standard lamp. He picked up the telephone. It was answered immediately.

"Mrs Harris," he said. "It's Henry Butterworth. It's about our Friday arrangement. What with the credit crunch and everything, I'm afraid I have some bad news."

As Long as it Takes
by Susan Haigh

Scottish Arts Club Short Story Finalist 2016

For Mireille, grief seems like an impossible dream.

Mireille Marie Maupeu knows about planes. If you were to ask her, she'd say she doesn't love planes, or even like them. Not at all. She has a passion for them; that's not the same; not the same at all. Planes fill her head, like bees burrowing into her brain – *that* bit of her brain. Then there's the smell: aviation fuel. That never leaves her, either.

Mireille Marie Maupeu has a job – an important job, she'd say. At the airport, it is, where they call her *Madame*, instead of Mireille. Or, even worse, Mie. She doesn't like people to call her Mie; it's disrespectful, childish, for a woman of her age – fifty-nine next birthday – a woman of her standing. They gave her this job because of her extensive knowledge; she's sure of that now. No, it's not only extensive, it's profound. In the years she has spent studying the skies, the arrivals boards, the gates, the passengers, she has seen everything. When she first came here, just after she'd heard, when it all started, she saw angels descending through mist, wings poised, landing on tip-toe on the runways, carrying messages of hope; but rarely now. More recently, she has seen winged chariots, trailing clouds of fire and foreboding across the skies; and eagles glinting in the sun, wings already spread, ready to soar on the high thermals. She knows their shapes, their colours – Air France, pristine white; the dancer's position of Ryanair; the green – oh, that tasteless, ugly green of Aer Lingus, she can't abide it; the red, white, blue of American Airlines. Mireille has watched; she has asked questions; she has wondered about the magic and mystery; she has tried to understand. How is it that a plane can stay in the sky? And sometimes it doesn't.

How? Why? She asks herself that every day. Her brain, *that* bit of her brain, the bit that's full of planes, won't let her think, let her *know*. And what happens to those people, if …?

She shrinks away from the words as they form in her mind, can't let them settle into the shape of her nightmares.

Each morning, at ten o'clock, Mireille Marie Maupeu leaves her post and walks across to the airport bar, where she sits at a table overlooking the runway. She twists her hands, pulls the skin on her wrists this way and that way, then pats her hair and sighs. The waitress smiles; a friendly smile. '*Madame*?' She knows how Mireille likes to be addressed. Madame does not look up. An expresso appears in front of her. She doesn't speak, but rummages in her waist-purse for change. Small change is all she has these days. Not like it used to be. She reaches out to drop the coins onto the tray on the table, but a hand on her arm stops her. This time she lifts her head to look at the waitress, who is smiling again and shaking her head. A croissant appears beside the coffee. Mireille lifts the cup to her lips, carefully, with both hands, shaking slightly, her eyes fixed on the runway. She watches as passengers make their way down distant steps and across the tarmac like ants, workers on the march.

For the half-hour of her break, Mireille Marie Maupeu stares out of the window at the highway rolling out into the skyline, as if it, too, might be taking off. She counts the people as they walk towards her. Wonders where they've come from, where they are bound for. Briefly, she sees her reflection in the window and turns her head away; then she gets up and walks back to her post. She sits down in her kiosk, looks up at each customer, smiles expectantly. Some smile back. Sometimes she holds out a small photograph. 'Where have you come from…?', 'Have you …?' she whispers. Some look confused. Mostly they ignore her. Occasionally, a face will lean down towards hers, '*Madame? Comment?*' She doesn't reply. Sometimes, a uniformed hand will rest on her shoulder for a moment, then move on. Coins appear in her saucer as her customers come out and hurry away to their own destinations and destinies.

Mireille keeps her trolley around the back of her block, well out of the sight of passers-by. She likes to keep things neat and that includes her trolley. Neatness is her job. She is proud of her work. Her customers have only the best; warm towels, hand-wash containers always full, each cubicle carefully inspected after use, toilet rolls neatly folded at the end. She looks after her block as if it were her own home.

Later, in the evening, she will make her way to the restaurant, always almost empty by the time she gets there; maybe a few couples, who take no notice of a middle-aged woman sitting alone by the window, always by the window. They won't see her unfold a piece of newspaper and peer at it. They won't see the faded photograph or the headline: *Air France plane loses contact over the Andes. A hundred and fifty passengers and six crew members missing.* But *she* will remember it, *that* day; the television report, the disbelief, the minutes that refused to pass, her skin turning to ice, her heart racing, out of control; then her husband's numbed stillness, the words that wouldn't come. Days later, more reports, rescuers were searching for the wreckage; then the lists – two lists. First the dead; then the missing. 'Missing'. Such a hard word, hard to understand, to take in, a word that seems to have – no end.

Then the years without news. But *she* had to go on, go on living – somehow – for him, for her son. She began to think that maybe, just maybe, somewhere … Miracles *have* happened; Mireille knows that.

Her husband, now ex-husband, didn't believe in miracles; got tired of hearing her talk about it after six years. Wanted them to be … *normal* … again, he said. Took her to a counsellor, who called her Mie – so disrespectful – told her she had to 'work through it', as if it were some kind of job or an exercise in a school text-book. How can you work through something when you don't know what it is you're working through? Told her she had to get past the first 'task'. Said it was denial. How could she get through *that*, never mind all the other so-called 'tasks' he talked about, when there wasn't anything *to* deny? She even had a spell of 'rest' in a clinic; time to reflect, they said.

By the time she got home again, *he* had gone, too, her husband. Left her some cash and a note. Said he was sorry. He couldn't listen any more, couldn't cope.

Then she found this job, the perfect job. And here she is, waiting. Waiting for her son. It doesn't matter how long; she'll wait however long it takes. No-one, *no-one* will ever say she gave up, didn't wait long enough, wanted her life, her mind back.

At twenty-three thirty hours, Mireille Marie Maupeu will take her trolley into her block, checking that everything is there, and close the door behind her. She will turn the key in the lock and take a final look around to see that everything is clean and ready for the morning customers; then she will undress and step into the shower. She will stand under the warm spray and feel *at home.*

At twenty-three forty-five, she will take her sleeping bag from her trolley – Carrefour, found abandoned in the airport car-park – and carefully spread it on the floor. Then, with equal care, she will take a parcel wrapped in a towel and remove a frame with a photograph of a young man in Air France uniform. She will place it on top of the cupboard where she keeps her cleaning materials; then she can see him, Mathieu Michel Maupeu, when she wakes up. She will lie down and try to sleep. Of course, what she would really like to do is to remove her own head for a while, and place it, too, with all its planes and noises and smells and questions not answered and imagined terror and pain and the time-bomb of her own grief, on the cupboard beside the photograph. Just for a while. Then she could rest, wouldn't be so exhausted in the morning.

She will get up at precisely four twenty, dress, comb her hair without looking in the mirror, roll up her sleeping-bag, return the photograph to the towel, tidy her trolley, unlock the door, push her trolley to the back of her block and watch the first planes glide down through the clouds. She will sit in her kiosk and she will wait – again; she will ask – again: *How? Why? Have you seen him, my son, Mathieu Michel Maupeu?*

Sheep Shape by
Michael Hamish Glen

Scottish Arts Club Member's Award Winner 2016

It began, like a B movie, with a phone call.

"Hullo, Gavin Prentice? This is Torquil MacKay, Inverclachan Estate Agents."

"Hi Torquil, good news?"

"Aye, maybe. That new road to the village, you know it cut off some of Willie Johnstone's land."

"Is he selling it?"

"No, Gavin. The council had to buy it and I'm selling it for them."

"How much and can I build on it?"

"That's the interesting bit. The land slopes steeply down from the road and Planning said they'd likely permit a house to be built into the hill. Even a contemporary one."

Gavin eyes sparkled. For years he'd wanted to keep sheep – he wasn't sure why. He'd retired from teaching languages and earned a few quid as a translator. He needed an antidote to converting bad English into good French.

"Torquil, you know my price limit."

"They'd be happy with 75K. It's only 15 hectares of pasture. Fine for your wee herd of sheep!"

Gavin sold the house where his wife had been born and had died from cancer. He bought the pasture-land from the council, commissioned a striking, passive-energy house and a landmark 'agricultural building'.

The rest of his life began with another phone call. Johnny Beaton, his architect, rang to say that both house and farm building were signed off for occupation.

Gavin had long contemplated names for his new demesne: perhaps Nirvana, Elysium or Tir nan Òg; maybe Paradise. But he wasn't Buddhist, Greek, Gael or even Persian, so he stuck to Scots and called it *Hamepairts*.

A week after moving in, he walked over to see Willie Johnstone. "Willie, I'm thinking of keeping sheep but I need lessons. D'you know anyone who'd help?"

Willie smiled indulgently. "Are ye efter earnin money or juist haein them as faimily?"

"More decoration than meat, to be honest. But I still need advice." Gavin felt rather foolish.

"My dochter's lowsed frae agricultural college and she's no got a job, except helpin hereaboots. Wad ye pey her?"

"Of course. And I'd enjoy having a youngster around. Would you ask her?"

That weekend, a lassie chapped Gavin's door. "Ah'm Sandra-Mae, Dad sent me ower."

Gavin, not a tall man, looked skywards to make eye-contact. "Come away in Sandra-Mae. Tea, coffee – or a dram?"

"Drinkin afore nuin? That's sinfu … a wee dram, please." Gavin warmed to her immediately. "It's my mam cries me Sandra-Mae. She got it frae a film. Dad cries me Lang Sandy acause of ma skinny legs an beaky neb like a heron."

"And a gleg ee, I'd jalouse. Pleased to meet you, Sandy." Gavin went to get the *Lagavoulin* and tumblers. "Your dad'll have told you I fancy keeping some sheep. I know it's mad, but can you help?"

"Och aye, an Ah'd like tae," she responded. "Ah did a module oan sheep-husbandry and it'd be guid experience. Hae ye a breed in mind?"

"Don't laugh, but yes," Gavin smiled. "Lleyns, these lovely woolly beasts from North Wales. And maybe some wee Shetlands. Would they run together?"

"Aye, nae probs. Lleyns yield a wheen o wool and they're prolific mithers, guid milkers, easy tae keep an grand tae eat. Shelties'll gie ye fine wool an smashin flesh. Jings, Ah soond like a catalogue," she laughed. "An Ah ken breeders o baith."

They fixed wages, purchased a score of gimmer shearlings, bought supplements and equipment, sorted out legalities and even chose names for the girls. Welsh ones for the Lleyns.

The agricultural building was 'heroic', the minister said. Gavin called it his *House of Four Winds* because its open cruciform shape provided shelter whatever the wind direction. The crowning glory, literally, was a glazed lantern which Willie named *Gavin's lookooterie*. "Be Robinson Crusoe," he said, "Maister o aw ye survey."

Gavin was slowly learning about sheep-rearing when one day Sandy arrived with her biggest smile so far. "Hae ye thocht o goats?"

"Never."

"A freend of dad's haes tae sell his Saanens – they're Swiss, like. An there's a billy. Ah thocht we micht sell their milk. An the Lleyns' milk as weel." Her enthusiasm was palpable.

"I like the 'we', Sandy," said Gavin, with amusement. "Aye, why not; but the ewes'll need tupping this autumn. And what about the regulations?"

"Och, we can extend the *Four Winds*. An get a lend o tups frae the fowk we bocht the yowes frae. An rules is nae problem."

Nothing, thought Gavin with pleasure, was a problem for Lang Sandy. And so they bought ten elegant white Saanen nannies and the well-hung billy. They adapted the *Four Winds* for kidding and lambing. Sandy sorted out the tupping and, together, she and Gavin planned their marketing.

"Janice's shop in the village, an the Castle shop, they'll sell the milk. Two hotels'll buy it an there's plenty ither retailers in these pairts. But we're wantin a name."

How about *Four Winds*? Gavin asked. With a picture for our logo.

"Ah'll buy that," said Sandy. "Or, mair tae the point, Ah'll sell that! Oh, Rona Paiterson will buy aw oor fleeces – she spins, felts, knits, weaves, an kens mony ithers in the Rural that dae as weel. It'll aw add up."

The months wore on and Sandy became a fixture at *Hamepairts*. She bubbled over with ideas and another soon arrived.

"Mam's feenished her part-time job an got bored. She's intae rhubarb jams an chutneys, so she's pit up a wee shed for makking them. An, forbye …" Gavin waited with baited breath. "She's wants us tae grow the rhubarb; she'll mak the preserves if we sell them as *Four Winds*. What d'ye think, mister?"

Gavin wondered if it was worth thinking because he felt, as ever, the die was cast – and he revelled in it. He knew Sandy would sort out the practicalities. She always did. He foresaw a lengthy calendar of lambing, kidding, rhubarb harvesting and whatever else for the months and years to come.

And come they did. With kids, lambs and wool. Milk, jam and chutney sales rose and income began to match spending. Gavin even marked 'abattoir' on the calendar.

Sandy turned up, animated, at seven one morning. "Gavin, ye ken dad's giein up fermin. He's convertin the steadin tae holiday hames but keepin the barn. He's hingin oan tae the truck tae fetch an cairy for ither fairmers, the JCB because there's aye fowk wantin tae hire it, an the pickup for me tae uise. An he's gettin a taxi licence for his new car." She drew breath.

"He'll not be busy then," joked Gavin.

Sandy added excitedly, "Oh, an he's lettin the land,"

Gavin was wise to Sandy. "Is that you hinting that we might rent it?"

"The thocht nivver crossed ma mind!" She giggled. "We maun gang intae partnership."

"I thought we had."

"Aye, but properly. An, by the way, we can extend the biggin for free-range chickens, geese an ducks. The butcher said he'd sell them nae boather, an the hotels aw want *Four Winds* poultry on their menus. Oh, an turkeys. Mair the merrier."

She paused. "Listen, ye never uise the lookooterie. It'd mak a cool doocot!"

"Help!" exclaimed Gavin, absorbing this.

"Ah'm awready helpin, ye gowk," Sandy chortled.

Many seasons went by. Poultry arrived and departed, 'slaughtered, de-feathered and eviscerated'. The *Four Winds* partnership prospered from its rented hay meadows, its barley and neep fields, its rhubarb patch – and its raggledy, taggledy assembly of trusted, rusted machinery. *Translation no more*, Gavin reflected.

But he started fretting. It was months since Sandy's last notion. However, next day, the kitchen door swung open and her highness marched in. "Man, ye're still at yer breakfast. Look at the time!"

"Good morning, sunshine. Tea? Coffee?

"Naw, Ah've juist had. Gavin, *Four Winds* is daein weel, Ah'm gettin a guid wage and ye're no starvin. But Ah wis thinking …"

"And when are you not, hen?" Gavin relished Sandy's company. "You'll be the death of me."

"Wrang chyce o wirds, Gav. Listen, ma brither Andy, he's a trained mortician – weel ye ken that – he's stairtin his ain business an wants tae dae green burials." Gavin groaned at what was coming.

"Yon field by the burn. Coud we no hae a wee burial grund there?" Another die was cast.

And so, one afternoon, ten years after Sandy cast her spell over Gavin, a solemn – if bizarre – procession passed *Hamepairts*. A JCB, clean for the first time since new, a hearse, a taxi and a pickup entered the green sward under the sign *Sheep May Safely Graze*.

Sandy dug a grave, Andy and his assistants lowered a wicker coffin and the local sculptor gently placed, as a headstone, her carving of a Lleyn. The inscription read, simply: 'sheep shape'.

The mourners raised glasses of Gavin's *Lagavoulin*.

Whit're ye gaun tae dae noo, lass? asked Sandy's mother.

"Weel, Gavin's left me *Hamepairts* an *Four Winds*. Ah'll juist hae tae find a man an raise a wee herd o weans. We'll be sheep shape, dinnae fash."

The Gannet
by Iain MacDonald

Winner, Scottish Arts Club Short Story Competition 2017,
Winner, Isobel Lodge Award, 2017

"If I went there a second time; it'd be as hopeless as the first."

This was the thought in Torvald's mind as he finished tying up his boat. The crab pots lay empty with mouths aghast showing hungry, netted bellies. A breath of exasperation came from the old fisherman's lips – the cracked skin on his chin like a road map of some forgotten kingdom. Finishing the knot, he stood up straight and stretched out of the weight of the day.

The sky was growing darker – night came and enveloped the day with an unstoppable lust. He took one last look at the sea – his provider – then turned his back and started walking up the hill. The sea sounded behind him, crashing against the shore like laughter.

The path was straight and led directly to where Torvald wanted to go; *The Shochad*.

He stuffed his hands into his wax coat pockets and lifted out his pipe. Once lit, the puffs of smoke became a fog around his head; a passerby would swear they had seen a ghost. As the small light appeared in the distance, he thought of the men inside and the smells and the sounds. George the crofter would be sat at the table to the right of the door reading a small book and occasionally you'd hear him scribbling down a note, as if his life and wife depended on it. What he wrote no one knew and he wasn't one for sharing. Seamag would be sat at the end of the bar, his head raised with a pained smile.

"My woman will be wantin' me home! This is my last one. Just one more for the ditch," he'd say. His wife, a fiery redhead called Halla, was a hell of a woman. Stony and ancient as if carved from ivory. Beautiful too, but that didn't matter much to Torvald.

There'd be Duncan and Willy, arguing about this or the other as siblings tend to do. The young mainlander, Patrick, who came over so long ago he hardly seemed like a mainlander anymore, or in fact, young. The bar man, a small tubby man they called 'Horse', would be expecting Torvald and have a dram waiting.

This is what kept Torvald warm as he walked the cold path. A man could forget a poor days fishing in *The Shochad* and dream of better ones.

So it was that Torvald came to the wooden door and pushed it open. Those familiar smells and sounds rushed out the door and he closed it quickly behind him, lest they be lost to the outside world forever. He stood in front of the door and observed the scene around him. The smell was toil and yeasty. The brothers Duncan and Willy hardly looked up from one another but gave him a welcoming nod.

George was sitting by the table to the right of the door, as predicted, and just by sensing his presence, he said, "Torvald." A book-reading man need not say much more in the way of a greeting.

The aforementioned Torvald approached the empty stool as Horse placed a dram on the bar top.

"Poor day at the crabs?" Horse asked, but knew the answer.

"When is it not?" George answered, on Torvald's behalf.

Before he could take the first sip to release the pain of the day, he heard Seamag's voice coming from the end of the bar, drifting over like syrup.

"Just this one for me and then I'm off, Torv. Halla will have the potatoes ready and the soup will be cold by now. I might have to suck it out through the earth. Again." Halla had been known to pour Seamag's dinner out the window if he came home pissed. He had had to fight many a dog for his supper.

Patrick, at a distance, exchanged pleasantries as Torvald began filling up his pipe with his calloused hands. He mentioned something about the mainland and a change which had come upon it. They spoke, but Torvald remained passive, as ever.

And this is how the night went on.

***

What surprised all the men after several hours of this relative normality was a loud thump against the wooden door of *The Shochad*. Torvald was first to raise his head as silence slowly fell upon the arguing brothers and scribbling scribe. George closed his book and placed it flat on the table. Although it may seem insignificant to most people, this thump at the door caused a mis-alignment in all these men that night. Torvald rose.

"What do you suppose that was?" Horse asked with slight hesitancy and fear.

The men looked around at one another. They looked like weary chess pieces.

"It wouldn't be Halla," Seamag asserted, bolting in with positive affirmation. "She'd never come and drag me home. That'd be too good for me!" What was to be one more drink had so far turned into four more.

Torvald led the wary crowd to the door and slowly pushed it open. As the door creaked open, it was clear the night had grown blacker and colder since he had made the short walk from his boat.

"Hmph!" He heard Patrick sound dismissively behind him.

As the men were ready to turn back and resume their night inside, Torvald glanced at his feet and saw the sprawled body of a gannet. Its huge wingspan spread, exposing its pearly white belly. Eyes open and black as night.

"A gannet," George stated with authority, some memory of ancient mythology in his crusty voice.

"Dead?" asked Duncan.

Torvald pressed his boot, gently, into its side. "Dead."

"It must have flown straight into the door," Horse suggested with an element of wonder and surprise.

"Birds at night," George pitched in. "An omen."

The men stood around that dead bird in an almost druidic silence. A silence that even the mystics would struggle to hear. It was as if all their silences, a lifetime's worth, had come at once for each of those men, crofters, fisherman, writer and brothers. An unstoppable hum of quietness, starting at their feet and travelling up through their bloated guts, choking their hearts.

Torvald looked around at the men – the only one moving was Seamag. He wept silent tears and his shoulders moved up and down, like a machine, obscuring the moon behind him as they rose and fell. All the men knew that Halla had died five years ago – Seamag never wanted to admit it to himself or any other.

"I'll get a shovel." Horse said; breaking the fragility as he turned and went back inside. Torvald stared into the gannet's black eye and saw the sea – beckoning him forward.

Kept from the Sea
by Kendal Delaney

Scottish Arts Club Short Story Commendation 2017

His shorts were wet with the salt water he had splashed out of the rock pools. A little unsteady, he straightened, turned and waved to his mother sitting on the beach behind him. Her skirt spread around her; the blue striking against the sand.

As he clambered over the next barnacle-covered rock, one sandaled foot slipped into the rock pool beneath, startling a shrimp which had been loitering in the shallower water.

He glared at the seaweed which had caused the trouble. Slimy and glistening, slug-like, it clung tenaciously to his calf, bandaging this latest scrape. Lip curled in disgust, he picked it off between forefinger and thumb and hurled it with determined effort at his sister, two rock pools behind.

Although it landed far short of her, he was satisfied by her squeal of surprise and disdain, his mouth tugging up at the corner in what his mother called his crooked smile.

He turned his attentions back to the pool; one foot still submerged. The shrimp had disappeared entirely but there was still much to look at: the rippling, undulating sea anemones; the cast-off shells of long-eaten creatures; tiny crabs with backs speckled like his marbling paper. The anemones were his favourite and he leaned in towards the largest. Its jellied flesh wonderful itself but the greatest joy came from hovering a finger above the flickering tentacles. Instantly pulling in its prey, the anemone grabbed the pad of the boy's finger. Wide-eyed, delighted, the boy pulled back his hand, ripping away from the many-fanged maw.

'Don't go too far' came his mother's voice from the sandy picnic dune. Startled, he stood and half-turned. Shielding his eyes, the boy twisted to find his sister. He spotted her at the edge of the cove; her long-legged form hoisting its way, crab-like onto the grass-strewn outcrop. They rarely played together. He acknowledged that she – three years older – was superior in both knowledge and experience and was, in consequence, sadly lacking in imagination.

The boy crouched once more by the pool. It was the biggest of the bay, broad and deep. A world entirely isolated, preserved and perfect between the tides. So much to see: the shimmering surface, puckered by the breeze and distorting what lay beneath. He remembered tales his grandfather had told him – ancient stories of selkies pining for the sea when hard-hearted humans had trapped them on land. He shuddered momentarily at the prospect of wicked men hiding away the pelts and their selkie wives weeping in horror and frustration.

Hoping to catch a glimpse of such a creature, he sank a second foot to follow the first and bent double so his nose was mere inches from the water. The boy was initially transfixed by the mottled discoloration of his skin; the cold turning his feet purple and white. Like radishes he thought as he wiggled his toes. He laughed.

The seaweed which caught his attention was remarkable for two reasons: the astonishing shade of brown was hard to describe and it was flashing in the sunlight, its undulating sheen seemingly alive. It was, of course, at the far end of the rock pool and the boy sighed with an explorer's determination and steeled himself to get very wet indeed. He would inevitably be scolded but the women in his family simply could not fathom the unbridled joy of being the first boy to step on new ground. Like Christopher Columbus, he crossed the sea, admittedly slipping a little on the green slime which coated the floor of the rock pool.

At the far end of the pool, and by now waist deep in water, the boy stopped and stared down at his find. So that was why the colour had seemed so striking. It was not seaweed at all; it was her hair. She was not a selkie. From his books at home, he knew she must be a mermaid. She was beautiful, her long hair caressing her face as she looked back up at him, entirely unafraid. He knew that she would not speak but her eyes were wide and curious – she was just as surprised to see him as he was her.

Careful not to scare her away, the boy crept to the side of the pool and shuffled onto a dry ledge, never taking his eyes off her. She, it seemed, had lost interest in him; her gaze still turned upwards, out of confinement.

It must be horrible to be stuck in such a tiny pool he thought, as the wind blew sparse clouds over the sun. Used to the freedom of the sea, she must be so afraid. He knew that the high tide would free her. He would have to stay until she was safe.

Minutes passed as he vigilantly kept his post. He was her knight, determined to protect her from dragons and treasure hunters and his sister. The water darkened as larger clouds followed the wisps of before. It was suddenly cold, so far from the residual warmth of the beach. The boy's mother called and beckoned as he looked around. He could not hear her words but he was tempted to scramble back to where there were hugs and hot drinks and dry clothes. Absent-mindedly, the boy began to crawl from his rocky chair.

She would not be alone for long.

It took the boy several minutes to pick his way back over the rocks. His mother had watched his sliding progress and was waiting with a towel as he leapt from the last of the rocks into the coarse, silver sand. She bundled the boy into her arms, swinging and tipping him in one of their favourite games. His bright laugh rang out to where his sister stood motionless by his rock pool.

The young boy's laughter seemed to break some reserve of courage in the girl and her scream startled not only her family but many others in the vicinity. He knew he should not have left her unguarded. His mother was by now too far ahead of him and he tried vainly to catch her to hold her back.

It was too late. The boy watched as his mother joined the other adults by the pool. She pulled his sister away. Shaking, crying, hands clasped, they scrambled back to him.

The boy struggled as his mother swung him onto her hip. He demanded to be put down but his mother did not hear him. He scowled at his sister who stalked, head bowed behind them. And then he cried for the mermaid who was being lifted from the water by grown men whose wives turned their faces away.

He wept because he knew the fate that awaited a mermaid kept from the sea.

Immortal Memory
by Peter Mallett

Scottish Arts Club Short Story Commendation, 2017

A guid New-year I wish thee, Maggie!
Hae, there's a rip to thy auld baggie:
Tho' thou's howe-backit, now, an' knaggie, I've seen the day
Thou could hae gaen like onie staggie Out-owre the lay.

"Sir, we can't understand it; that's not proper English!"

The same complaint every year. I always give the fifth form this poem at the end of January. Burns' birthday. A good time to remember the past as well as look forward to what the future may bring. Some of the fathers of the current bunch studied Burns with me in this same room. Their initials are probably carved on the rows of wooden desks arrayed before me, memorials to an earlier era. Nothing much has changed in the thirty years I've been teaching here; Hawkeswood Hall doesn't believe in modernization. I sometimes feel as though I've awoken to find myself in a shabbier version of the room I went to sleep in decades before. Only the pupils' hairstyles have changed – and their infringements of the uniform rules. White socks are the current fad.

"As Blackstone has informed us: it's not 'proper English'. So what is it?" I look hopefully along the rows of adolescents slouched over their desks in that bored 'whatever' attitude teenage boys have. "Andrews?"

"Dialect, sir?"

"Good. Any guesses which dialect?" This elicits a better response. I choose a hand at the back of the class.

"Scottish?"

"That's right. Lowland Scots. And which poet wrote in Lowland Scots? Chapman?"

"Robert Burns."

"Well done. So what's it about? Who's Maggie?"

"Is she his girlfriend, Sir?"

"No, Mullers."

"Not his girlfriend, Mullers, you dumbo; his wife. Look, he calls her an old bag!"

"Thank you, Rawthorne. Any advances on 'wife'?"

Blank stares all round. "Look at the title: *The Auld Farmer's New Year Morning Salutation to his Auld Mare, Maggie.*"

"It's a horse! Maggie's a horse."

"That's right, Browning."

There's a mini-conference in the third row. "But what's 'howe-backit' and 'knaggie', Mr Johnson?"

"Maggie's old now and misshapen – hollow-backed and knobby." Sniggers.

I know what they're thinking. The arrogance of youth – old age is the preserve of their grandparents, even their parents. Nothing to do with them.

O life! How pleasant, in thy morning,

Young Fancy's rays the hills adorning!

But I was no different at their age. I also imagined my days stretching into a limitless future where senility did not exist. If only they knew how quickly their time will pass! My skin was once soft and supple like theirs, my hair – not much of it remaining – jet black and thick. My arms, now *knaggie*, once bowled for the school cricket team.

Unthinkable to these teenagers, I, like Burns, once experienced romance and passion.

"Is it a metaphor, sir?"

Thank God for one bright spark. There's one in every class, someone to make this job worthwhile. "Go on, Potts."

"The poem seems to be about an old horse. But it's really about the farmer, isn't it, and the passing of time?"

"Exactly." I offer a silent prayer of gratitude that this pupil will carry Burns' legacy to the next generation. "The farmer's probably in his fifties. Quite old for the period. Remember, Burns was only 37 when he died."

I've been teaching Burns longer than Burns lived.

"As Potts has pointed out, the poem's about the human condition. How time passes and we all change – yes, even you, Mullers, you'll find you're not immortal. The farmer remembers Maggie as a sleek, grey young mare twenty-nine years before when he was courting his future wife."

When first I gaed to woo my Jenny.

Dead now six years, my own Jenny. No one teaches you in school that one day you may be on your own; it's not a natural condition. I've always been part of a family. I met Jenny at university; we married soon after graduating. Two children quickly followed. In forty years of marriage I hardly ever had the house to myself. I never expected I'd be the surviving partner. *Widower.* Possibly the only word in the English language for which the masculine is a suffixed form of the feminine.

We've worn to crazy years thegither;

We'll toyte about wi' ane anither;

No one for me to totter about with. Even the dog's gone. They don't live as long as horses, we couldn't grow old together. No point in getting another one now, I'd be 80 before a new puppy was a mangy old dog.

The house is all that remains of a life lived together. Number 46 Elm Drive has aged and frayed with me, a museum of the changing fashions of interior design. The Ercol bentwood furniture we bought when we first married is still serviceable; back in the 50s it was trendy but things were made to last then, not like today's disposable goods. Perhaps there'll be a revival and it'll enjoy new popularity as a retro-look. The bathroom was renovated in the 70s – pink suite; the kitchen in the early 80s – orange tiles and pine dresser. Nothing much since. The house will see me through.

91

"Sir?"

"Sir!!"

***

"Eddie?"

I sometimes wonder whom she's addressing. No one ever called me Eddie before. As a schoolboy, I was 'Edward', as an adult 'Mr Johnson' – at the least. Mostly 'sir'. Funny how respect decreases in proportion to your age in this country. In some cultures, the old are valued.

"Been sleeping again, have we?"

Well, I have, not much else to do in this place. I can't vouch for Mrs Bullock (no first names allowed there, note), chief cook and bedpan emptier. She hasn't yet realized the two activities are not unconnected: if her cooking were better, the bedpans would need emptying less often.

"It's time for our medicine."

I'm not sure when Mrs Bullock assumed joint ownership of my prescription. "I think I'll give it a miss today. You have it for me, Mrs Bullock."

"Oh, you're in good form today, aren't you, Eddie? Well, don't play around, it's nearly time for our bath."

Since when did Mrs Bullock get to share the tub with me? I haven't been bathed by anyone since my mother scrubbed me at the age of seven. Shakespeare was right: *Last scene of all that ends this strange eventful history is second childishness*. I graduated from Shakespeare's sixth age – *the lean and slipper'd pantaloon, with spectacles on nose and pouch on side* – as soon as they brought me in here. It won't be long now till *mere oblivion* follows.

"Now come along. I'll park you here next to Mrs McLeod so you can watch *Eastenders* together. Aileen, this is Mr Johnson. I think you'll have a lot in common. Eddie's quite a reader. Used to be a teacher, I heard."

Why does she talk about me as though I'm not here? Just because I'm old, doesn't mean I can't hear. Does not mean I'm stupid.

"You're the new inmate, aren't you, Mrs McLeod?"

"Resident, Eddie. Resident."

"Yes, Mrs Bullock. Resident."

"I'll leave you two to get acquainted."

"Is that Burns you're reading, Mr Johnson?"

"That's right, Mrs McLeod. Do you like Burns?"

"Yes indeed, Mr Johnson. Today's his birthday, too."

"Twenty-fifth of January, so it is! Not that Mrs Bullock thinks fit to honour the occasion. Though I wouldn't fancy my chances with her haggis."

"Definitely a risk not worth taking. I'm sure the combination of Mrs Bullock's cooking and non-stop *Eastenders* is going to finish me off one day."

"What was your crime then, Mrs McLeod?"

"Corruption of the Waterworks Department. Petty Piddling of Noxious Liquids. And yours?"

"Breaking and Entering."

"Breaking and Entering?"

"Yes, broke my hip and entered the County General Hospital. No-one to look after me when I was released."

"No children?"

"My son's working abroad; my daughter's in the west country. Job, family; no time to look after an invalid. How about you, Mrs McLeod?"

"Daughter, only child. Chief witness, prosecutor and judge in the case. Did they give you a life sentence too?"

"Seems more like a death sentence."

"When ance life's day draws near the gloamin, Then fareweel vacant, careless roamin."

93

"Burns. He knew what he was talking about, Mrs McLeod."

"He did indeed. The whole of human experience compressed into thirty-seven short years. Well, why don't we have our own little celebration of the Bard? Will you take a wee dram with me to toast the Immortal Memory? I happen to have a stash of miniature malt samples secreted away."

"Strictly against the rules, Mrs McLeod."

"Exactly. And all the tastier for it."

"Leeze me on thee, John Barleycorn, Thou king of grain!"

"You know, Mr Johnson, I think you and I are going to get on very well together.

Come and park your wheelchair over in my room!"

"Are you making improper suggestions, Mrs McLeod?"

"Absolutely, Mr Johnson. Let's age disgracefully together!"

Extracts from *The Auld Farmer's New-Year Morning Salutation to his Auld Mare, Maggie; Scotch Drink;* and *Epistle to James Smith* from the *Complete Poems and Songs of Robert Burns,* Lomond Books, Glasgow (2000)

Quotation from *As You Like It* (Act II, scene vii) by William Shakespeare: The Oxford Dictionary of Quotations, Book Club Associates by arrangement with OUP (1981)

The Magic of the Matinee
by Andrew Preskey

Scottish Arts Club Short Story Finalist 2017

I must have looked a right mess. I'd had a shower at the pithead, of course, but we were working unusual shifts to get the new equipment bedded in, which meant I didn't have time to go home and change. Not that we had many different outfits to change into in those days – work clothes, overalls, one set of casuals and Sunday best.

Well, I turned up straight from a day at the coal face, empty snap tin and flask in hand. I can tell you, she was not impressed! I still remember the course she was running, *The Poetry and Prose of Gerard Manley Hopkins*. Mind you, while she may not have been best pleased to have folk coming to her Adult Ed class looking like rejects from the local pit, she was quick enough to react when one of the other students commented about miners 'knowing their place'.

I can recall it now as if it were yesterday; she didn't reply as such, just calmly recited Wilfred Owen's poem – you know the one I mean, 'Miners'. The room went quiet; you couldn't even hear the sound of breathing. When she'd finished, we simply sat there gawping until this old fellow at the back started clapping and then the chap who'd made the remark joined him and then the whole room was applauding.

That's what makes it so sad. Some say she was the best English Teacher St. Martin's Secondary ever had; now she can't write her name. She can read a little – though, again, I'm not sure what the words mean to her anymore. Still, I wouldn't change a moment. Marrying Beth was the best thing I ever did, the most wonderful day of my life.

Our youngest, Ruth, keeps talking to me about care, "You know, Dad, you can't go on like this for ever – we all love Mum but it's not getting any easier." The lass means well, of course. Over to our place every other day to lend a hand, she always has us round for Sunday tea. It gives Beth a change of scenery – *and* me a rest from cooking duties! Still, there's no way Beth is going to live anywhere but home. She guaranteed that on our third date. We'd gone to the matinee showing *Calamity Jane*, probably because it was cheaper. I was a big, hardy coal miner in those days but, when Doris Day started singing *Secret Love* I quite welled up. Beth laughed; she squeezed my hand and whispered, "I *do* love you, Mike Lister."

Well, best press on, no time for reminiscing this morning. It's shower day today; I need to be getting her up and ready to face the world. It's funny, we had a shower put in about eight years ago when my arthritis started getting bad – too many rough tackles playing for the pit football team, I reckon. Anyway, it must be the best part of a decade since we had a bath in the house and yet the shower is always a surprise for Beth. She simply adores it, just like a little girl. I suppose, in that sense, this disease isn't all bad but I can't say it's been easy for either of us. It's not what you'd think; the practical stuff, household chores and the like, isn't a problem. No, what I miss most is her conversation – you know, being able to talk.

"Come on, love, through here. My, you do look smart after that shower. There's a cup of tea for you on the table and I'll have your breakfast ready in no time."

"For me?"

"Yes, you sit there on the yellow stool – your usual place."

And she does, for a minute, but after a sip of tea she is up again. She'll have noticed a bit of muck I've missed on the carpet or perhaps seen a brightly-coloured bird in the garden and she's off, breakfast not even a memory.

"Come and sit down, love. Fruit salad and a slice of toast with that lovely local honey – deee-licious," I say.

She turns and looks at the carefully prepared fresh fruit, always her favourite.

"For me?"

"Yes, and is there honey still for breakfast?" I ask, smiling at her.

Five years ago, perhaps even three, my mangling of Rupert Brooke's fine words would have met with a sharp riposte. Beth laughs tentatively. Despite the illness, she remains socially aware. I guess, some things are just so deeply ingrained. I remember the first time I noticed that about her. I'd chased her for weeks before she'd even consider a date with me; I'm not a big-headed sort but I couldn't understand why. She wasn't seeing anyone else.

"I could *never* go out with a man called Lister – think about it," she teased.

"Why ever not? It's a great old name, been in the family for years!"

"It's not that but, if we ever did get together, what kind of nickname do you think the kids would invent for an English Teacher called B. Lister?"

It had never occurred to me. Still, like they say, 'opposites attract'. Even now, as I gently rib her about breakfast, though Beth doesn't understand my quip, she's sensed that I'm joking. I smile at her and grab a spoonful of my porridge but, before I have swallowed it, the doorbell chimes.

"Who's that?"

"Don't worry, love. You finish your breakfast, I'll get the door," I reassure her.

It's Maggie, the special nurse. There are so many different medical folk these days, I forget her proper title – she does the photographs. It's like a cross between a memory box and a photo album, I guess, but it brings Beth a lot of pleasure. They seem to have unearthed all sorts of snapshots, scenes I'd long since forgotten – like when her friend, Sylvia, got married on that windy day in Calow and the wedding dress blew up over the bride's head. Funny, it's always the old pictures that seem to hold most meaning.

I leave them to it. Back in the kitchen, I bin my cold porridge, put the kettle on to make a cuppa and begin to wash up.

"Mr Lister?"

"Mike."

"I'm sorry, Mike, Beth has become a little agitated and I can't make out what is wrong."

I follow the nurse through to the lounge but I fear I already know the problem. "It's OK, Beth, I'm here now," I say, placing my hand over hers. She is clutching the picture as though her life depended upon it. And, in one sense, it may. Certainly, mine does.

"Come on, love. It's alright."

Beth looks at me, tears in her eyes. "Norman," she says, "But I think he's dead now."

She's right. He was on the coal face with me. That's what men did in our part of Derbyshire. It was one of those fluke accidents you get in pits. We'd done everything by the book, no skimping, no bodging. Norman, 'Big Norm', as we called him, wouldn't have stood for anything else. Simple thing, a prop failed. He hit me so hard barging me out of the way that it cracked two of my ribs. The roof fall broke his neck. Of course, we got him out. Dug through the mess with anything we could lay our hands on. But he died the next month, three weeks before his nephew was born, Norman Michael Lister.

"That's right, love. He was your big brother – my best man. Do you remember?" "Best man?"

"When we got married. *What* a day," I say, slipping a snap of the happy occasion into her other hand Beth stares at the picture, recognition and joy replacing the sadness in her face. Maggie looks on with a mixture of relief and understanding. Yes, it hasn't been a chocolate-box life we've had but then who gets that?

After the shower and the nurse's visit, we have a pretty routine day planned. There's a bit of chicken breast with some boiled pots and veg for lunch; then I grab us a couple of ice-creams from the freezer. I've already set up the DVD, while Beth was finishing her first course. So, here we are, two old folk with their choc-ices just waiting for the matinee showing. I press the remote and immediately the titles scroll up, *Seven Brides for Seven Brothers*.

Then, "Bless your beautiful hide …" Beth is singing along in perfect harmony and, again, I gratefully accept the miracle that somehow music has succeeded where words have failed. Gently, I take her hand.

It must be the third time we've watched this film together this month. I don't know whether they had better songs in those days or if it is simply the magic of the matinee, but some things I never seem to tire of hearing.

"I *do* love you, Mike Lister," she says.

Yes, some things I simply never tire of hearing.

Fish Suppers
by Susan Gray

Scottish Arts Club Short Story Finalist 2017

The sun was rising at the top of the Great Glen, a pink glow behind Ben Nevis. Eric looked up the loch, and said, "Bother! It's going to be a clear day."

Einmar peered out from the comfort of the nest at the top of the tree. "What's wrong with that?" she asked.

"Honestly, Einmar, have a think, will you? It's going to be sunny. It's nearly a Bank Holiday – guess who'll be coming to call?"

"Who?"

"Goodness me, Einmar, does that stupid tag on your wing not remind you about anyone?" "Oh yes – that bird man."

"Correct. And blow me, here he comes already. Where are Peter and Inga?"

"Out practising flying. I won't get them back in time to hide. And anyway Eric, you're too fat to lurk behind the branches."

Eric tried unsuccessfully to suck in his abdomen, nearly falling off the branch in the process. They watched the high-speed rib approaching from Oban, men clinging to their seats as it bucketed over the outgoing tide. It cruised along the shore, the occupants scanning the coast with enormous binoculars. Einmar was pushing the youngsters back into the nest, but it was too late. With a final snarl, the boat circled into the small bay, the engine noise bouncing off the rocks and disturbing a family of otters who were taking advantage of Eric's late rising habits by doing some early fishing.

"Bloody RSPB man," the mother said, snatching her brood and diving beneath the surface.

One of the men stood up, holding a large loudhailer, while trying to keep his binoculars to his eyes with the other hand.

"Oh God, it's that pest Rupert again," Eric said.

"Ahoy there, Eric! Don't be coy, we can see you!" the man shouted. Eric flapped a wing wearily in acknowledgement.

"How's the new tag doing?" Rupert continued. "Is it staying on any better?"

Eric adopted a cod Scandinavian accent. "Oh yes, Rupert. And I particularly like the bright emerald colour. Certainly tones in."

"Can we drop the Norwegian act, Eric?" Rupert went on. "You're Scottish now. You were always Scottish."

"No I wasn't. My dad's from Stavanger. Forcibly transported, I might add, worse than an Australian convict."

"Well, it would help things if you tried. Have you learned any Gaelic yet?"

Einmar sat down hastily on the shreds of Gaelic dictionary which had been used to line the nest.

"No I have not," Eric said. "I am not a Celt, I am Norse, Eric Ericsson, and my children will be Norse too."

"Well, let's leave that just now." Rupert tried a different tone. "We were wondering if you could help out this weekend?"

"Let me see, English Bank Holiday, is it? And I thought we had a deal, Rupert." Rupert's binoculars wobbled. "Well, I know …"

"Burn out, I was suffering from, Rupert. In and out for all those flipping boatloads at Jura, never a moment's peace before the next lot arrived, all those long lenses – worse than being Brad Pitt."

Einmar sniggered in the background. He rounded on her. "And you can keep quiet – you never had to do it – cushy number I got you here."

"Ah yes Eric, perhaps not so much burnout as a very messy divorce, I seem to recollect," Rupert said.

"Messy divorce? I was a saint with that bird. And it was an arranged marriage. Then you send over nice young birds like Einmar and what's a fellow to do?"

Eric fluffed out his chest feathers. "And I kept my end of the bargain. I have hardly touched a lamb since we moved here."

"That's as maybe, Eric, but we had an agreement you would do a scheduled number of flyovers. Have you got the Calmac timetable?"

"Yes, and I have been doing them. Now and then."

"Sightings are down, Eric. We are losing out to the whales. They've even lined up orcas on the east coast now. VisitScotland are threatening to cut our budget."

"Well, I can't help it if they have overactive whales. Couldn't you harpoon a few? And what's in it for me anyway?"

"It's always the deal with you, Eric. No empathy for your fellow birds."

"None at all, mate. The Donald Trump of the Western Isles, I am. Oh look, there's a ferry going by behind you. Looks like I've missed that one. Never mind." Eric settled back on his perch.

"We could relocate you again."

Einmar squawked in dismay. Eric spread his wings menacingly. "Don't even think of threatening my family."

Rupert looked desperate. "So what would you suggest?"

Eric thought. "Fish suppers," he said. Einmar flapped in agreement. "One per fly past, dropped from the ship's cafeteria."

"In a box, and a bag for carrying," Einmar added. "Nice lining for the nest. And no food preparation."

Rupert and his colleague had a quick discussion. "That might be possible," he said.

"I think it had better be possible." Eric spread himself out to his full wingspan. "Let's start tomorrow, shall we? Today's flights will be for free." With some preliminary limbering up, he took off from the branch, which bounded upward, almost catapulting Einmar into the air. She watched him appreciatively.

"Look at him go," she said.

Certainly, in the air, in full flight, Eric did lose some of the turkey-like appearance he had on land. He soared out over the firth, and headed towards Mull, catching the thermals higher and higher, until he was a distant dot.

"I do hope he comes down a little – stretching the long lenses a bit up there," Rupert commented.

"Of course he will," Einmar said. "He's a professional."

The summer passed, and the October half term brought the autumn migration of tourists, all eager to watch the eagle sweeping in for his plastic prey, scooped from the wake of each passing ferry. Einmar did worry a little about weight gain, but really it was so convenient, and she could always pop out to the fish farm if they needed something fresh.

In the spring a herring gull out of Oban delivered the new timetable. "Just a minute," Eric said. "There's more ferries now."

"RET mate," the gull said. "Hadn't you heard? They've made the crossing cheaper, so the tourists are flocking over to Mull like bloody starlings. They've had to bring the *Coruisk* down from Mallaig."

"I'll be suffering from burnout again soon," Eric complained, but Einmar hoped the extra flying would return her husband to the shape which had first lured her into his nest. There was a new brood to feed, and the extra fish was really very handy.

Down in Gourock, an assiduous accountant was entering all these fish suppers into a ledger, under sea eagle expenditure.

Once something is down on paper, it can only be so long before someone in authority gets to hear of it. Eric and Einmar were enjoying a happy afternoon of summer sunbathing between his shifts, when they saw a fast Fisheries cutter roaring up to the entrance to Loch Linnhe. An inflatable was lowered, and a man was ferried to the shore. He stepped carefully onto the shingle, clutching a briefcase to his chest. "Eric Ericsson? And Mrs Ericsson?" he said. HMRC,"

"Who?" Eric asked. "You'll have to be quick, I'll be off to the next ferry in a minute."

"Exactly," the taxman said. "You have been receiving benefits in kind for some time now, without making any declaration on a tax return."

"I didn't know a fish supper was taxable," Eric said.

The man laughed. "Everything is taxable. And you are very much in arrears."

Tears were beginning to drip down Einmar's beak. "We don't have any money," she said.

"I can only suggest that you take up some salaried employment extremely quickly," the taxman said. "Have the RSPB no funding?"

"They're concentrating on ospreys this year," Eric said gloomily. "And golden eagles. They've a new relocation scheme in Dumfries – costing over a million."

"Well, then, how about the private sector?" the taxman asked. "You could try the Majestic Line, new outfit, out and about in this area."

Eric had seen the little converted trawlers rolling up and down the loch, had even given them a few free flybys. "They're certainly local," he said. "But perhaps a bit small fry? I'm thinking more along the lines of the *Hebridean Princess*. A well-heeled clientele, only one cruise a week."

"Excellent," the taxman said. "I happen to know they already have a deal in place with minke whales off Coll. It should be pretty easy to set something up. They can open a bank account for you in Oban and we'll just get a direct transfer."

So it was that. Occasionally, the fish suppers bobbed uncollected in the wake from the *Isle of Mull*. Those were the nights when Eric and Einmar had sunset dinners of smoked salmon and monkfish, or perhaps a little Dover sole. No batter, so much better for the waistline

Silent Night
by Jonathan Lee

Scottish Arts Club Short Story Finalist 2017

That night Mum and I went to see Miss Reiner's production of *Jesus Christ Superstar*, which I was too young to be in, but was advertised through posters in our school dining room as a year-end extravaganza – for all ages.

According to a cutting I have kept from the time, the *Dumfries Chronicle* dubbed it 'the High School's most ambitious show to date', and for many it was also the most controversial. Graeme Henderson, who played Judas Iscariot, told me that Miss Reiner, our new Head of Music and Drama, had already received seven complaints before rehearsals had even started. Surely it was inappropriate to perform a show about Jesus's death but had nothing about his birth, especially at this time of the year for God's sake? Wasn't it true that a famous bishop had once called a Hollywood movie by the same name blasphemous? Wasn't this the very opposite of suitable for all ages?

It was well known that several complaints had come from parents unhappy about the influence our new music teacher was having on their children. According to Peter Lipsel, who played the Apostle Peter, this was because Miss Reiner had once been an actress in a morally dubious film in the early seventies, though no one in school was ever able to verify this. For her part, Miss Reiner, who was a good friend of my mother's through the Amateur Dramatic Society and often came to our home, said she never understood any of it. She had no qualms about her past and she only wanted her pupils to enjoy music and question things. She certainly had nothing against God. "I believe in him too," she told us.

Although Miss Reiner's defence was vigorous, her most ferocious critic continued to be Mr Baxter our Maths teacher. He was an Elder at St Leonard's and from what I could gather from snippets of my parents' conversations, the vociferous ringleader of the detractors. He ran a Bible club after school. I went to it once with Brian Hardy, who told me his mother forced him to go every week. The week I attended Mr Baxter recounted the story of Sodom and Gomorrah from the book of Genesis. He told us that the people's sin was so abominable that God rained burning sulphur on them, engulfing whole communities in a baptism of flames. Almost everyone was destroyed. "Almost" he repeated, raising a solitary finger towards heaven for emphasis. I found the story impossible to believe and never went back to Mr Baxter's club, much to his apparent dismay.

Despite the complaints and furious letters to the headmaster, *Superstar* proceeded as planned on the last day of term and Mum declared that she would show her support by buying Miss Reiner some flowers. That afternoon the assembly hall was so packed our janitor Mr Moffat ran out of chairs and late-coming parents were forced to sit squinting on window ledges from the far end. Emma Johnston, who played Mary Magdalene, unquestionably the most beautiful girl in our school, stood on a box under a pale spotlight and sang a solo about not knowing how to love a man. I turned to my mother mid-song and saw her dabbing her right cheek with a tissue.

The show, as the *Dumfries Chronicle* states, was 'a triumphant vindication of Miss Reiner's convictions'. At the finale, the whole assembly hall stood and applauded as fake military men with plastic machine guns walked off stage and Brian Humphries, who played Jesus, ascended into heaven in a pyrotechnic puff. Miss Reiner appeared on stage at the end, cried a little and kissed me on the cheek when I handed her the flowers.

Mum and I walked the long route home that night under an icy sky, our breaths appearing like cartoon balloons. It was only four days till the Big Day and I began thinking about relatives from faraway places descending on our home for turkey and paper hats and the Queen's Speech. I thought of Miss Reiner too, winding her way along the A709 to the village she lived in twelve miles away. I imagined her playing the *Superstar* soundtrack full blast as she drove, singing every lyric in triumph.

At last Mum and I turned into our road, walking past familiar windows illuminated with fairy lights and plastic Santas on front doors. At the end of our street lived the Hobarts, who had constructed, as they did every year, a life-size nativity scene in their front garden, complete with lowing oxen. Two silver angels guarded their front gate, trumpets pointing upwards, anticipating the moment when something unexpected might once again appear from the clouds. For a few seconds I thought I heard the sound of thunder and then a distant flash – a momentary flare illuminating the night sky. It made me think of Mr Baxter at Bible Club.

"One day Jesus will return you know, but it will be different next time. He won't come back as a baby in a manger. No. This time it will be in righteous holy anger and, believe me, it will be ten times worse than Sodom and Gomorrah. You'd better be right with God, for that day will be truly terrible."

When we returned to the house, I noticed the television was on in the living room. I pushed the door open and saw Dad standing frozen on the sheepskin rug, staring at the TV. On the screen was a passport-sized photo of a man who worked in a garage, his accent was local, saying, "Aye, like a fireball fallin frae the sky." A rolling ticker tape appeared with an emergency number to call.

Mum walked in behind me and said, "What is it?"

Dad shook his head. It was strange to see him like this, a tall brave man, stupefied against a backdrop of twinkling lights and angelic cards floating on the mantelpiece. He pointed to the screen. As the local man continued to talk a photo appeared of a village high street on a sunny day. I instantly recognised it. At the far end of the high street was a war memorial with a statue of an angel on top. Beneath it two young women with ponytails and crop-tops pushed prams along the pavement.

"What's happened?" Mum said, her voice now agitated.

Dad didn't answer. A man appeared from a TV studio in Newcastle. He was bald and wore a blue blazer with gold buttons. The presenter called him an Aviation Expert.

The presenter said, "Is it possible that this could be what some are saying it is?"

The Aviation Expert had a face like slate. "Yes," he said, "in my opinion, it is."

"Planes don't just fall out of the sky."

A photo of a Boeing 747 was shown and a map of Europe. A yellow arrow hopped from Frankfurt to London. Then it moved straight up to Scotland before coming to rest like a Christmas star above a village twelve miles from our home.

Mum started saying "Oh my God" over and over.

Dad said, "you'd better call her," and Mum rushed into the hallway and started spinning numbers into the plastic dial on the phone. She dialled and re-dialled, and re-dialled again, then stopped abruptly, her face pale.

"I can't get through," she said. "The line's dead."

The news presenter appeared once more. "We have been receiving reports tonight that at five minutes past seven, air traffic control lost all contact with Pan Am Flight 103 travelling from Frankfurt to Detroit. We have also heard multiple eyewitness accounts of a huge explosion over the town of Lockerbie. Emergency Services are at the scene and have appealed for the public to stay away from the area."

I stood by the fireplace unable to move, thinking this was impossible to believe. For the second time that night my Mum started to cry.

Twenty years later I am still haunted by the inverted series of events that night. My obsession has led me to keep hundreds of magazine articles and newspaper cuttings from the time that I still keep in a box at home. Most of them cover well-worn topics on Libyan politics, airport security and Scottish legal matters. But the piece that means most to me, the one I still read religiously every year, is page fifteen of the *Dumfries Chronicle* from 28 December 1988Though a little frayed now and yellow with age, it contains a short but fitting tribute to Miss Cassandra Reiner, including a photo taken backstage of her receiving one final ovation from a rapturous assembly hall forty-seven minutes before she was gone. And if I take a magnifying glass and look very closely, I can just about make out the blurred faces of my mother and me standing four rows from the front of the stage, clapping and cheering like fanatics, as if Miss Reiner's life depended on it.

Snake Bite
by Michael Callaghan

Scottish Arts Club Short Story Finalist 2017

I wave to my dad as he drives off and push open the door of the library. It's heavy and I have to use both hands to move it. It opens with a low, scraping, groaning noise; like it was asleep and I've disturbed it and it *really* didn't want to open. When I finally get in and let it go it slams behind me with a loud echoing bang.

I wince. Everyone knows that noise is a *baaad* thing in a library.

It's the first time I've been here. I like old buildings, especially old library buildings. I like the high ceilings and the big arched windows and those grainy white wall tiles. I like the stillness and the quiet and that rich, dark-brown smell of wood and leather and old paper.

Maybe that's why the kids at school think I'm weird.

As I walk on, I see three posters on the left wall. The first says what to do if there is a fire alarm. The second gives the opening hours. It's the last one that catches my attention. It's a POLICE NOTICE, warning people to be on alert. It shows a hand drawn picture of a man. He has a mean, thin-eyed, expression and a stubbly chin. It's not a very good picture – it doesn't look like any real-life person – but before I can read the notice I hear a cough. Not a real cough, like when you have a cold or something catches in your throat. It's a can-I-have-your-attention cough.

I turn and see the librarian. He's standing behind a long, horseshoe-shaped wooden desk, staring at me. I wonder how long he's been looking at me. He has a grey, scraggy beard that looks oddly patchy – like someone has pulled bits out of it – and silver rimless glasses that are too small for his face. He smiles, but in an odd way. Like something's going on in his head. It strikes me that he might be the sort of man that my dad tells me to be careful of.

But my dad worries too much.

"Can I help you … Sonny?"

He pauses before he says *Sonny*, and he pronounces his esses in a funny way. Slightly too long. It reminds me of the snake in *Jungle Book*; the one that pretends to be all nice to Mowgli – even while he's wrapping his coils round him. Tighter and tighter. Getting ready to *snap*.

"I just want to read a book, Mister," I don't smile back.

He makes a sad face.

"A book? Oh *dear*. I'm afraid you *can't* take books out unless you're a member. And you can't be a member unless you've got identification and one of your parents okays it."

I make my own sad face. "I don't want to take a book out. I just want to read a book. Here. My dad told me to come in here."

This is true, but that seems to trouble him even more. He rubs his top lip with his forefinger. It looks like he's rubbing off spit.

"All alone?" he says finally. "What age are you, I wonder? Nine?" He's started to talk very quietly. Like he's talking to himself.

"Ten."

"Ten? Hmm…" He looks behind me, to the wall. I turn and realise he's looking at the POLICE NOTICE.

"I'm surprised at your dad. Hasn't he told you about the … disappearances?"

(… *disssappearanccesss* …)

"We're new here," I say. "Just moved this week. What disappearances?" But before he can answer I say, "My dad was just going to Asda. He dropped me here and said he'd be about an hour and then he'd be back for me."

"About an hour? That so." He nods, like he's thinking, and does the lip rubbing thing again. "Well … you may as well know … some children have gone missing. Unpleasant business. It's got everyone quite … uptight," he gives his odd smile when he says the word 'uptight' for some reason. As if it's funny that people are uptight. Then he sighs.

"Well I don't think I want to send you back out if you're on your own. Not with all this, ahem, *business* going on." He flicks his head in the direction of the back of the library. "The children's section is at the back. No *Harry Potters* left but you might find a *Percy Jackson*."

He lowers his eyes to something in front of him, and then, like an afterthought, raises them once more. "And don't worry. You're safe here. I'll look after you." And he smiles that smile again.

I shrug and walk past him. It's early, and the main library is mostly empty, save for a homeless man who has his head down on a desk, asleep, and a woman reading a magazine and making shushy noises to a buggy she's rocking. There is indeed a children's section at the back. It's not very big. There are four book cases, five green plastic seats, and a small table with drawing paper and crayons.

I scan the shelves, looking for an Alex Rider, I don't really like Percy Jackson – and that's when I see the little boy.

He is wearing a cartoon t-shirt, it shows SpongeBob hugging his friend Patrick with the caption *Best Friends!* underneath, and pale blue cotton shorts. He is sitting at one of the tables, reading a *Thomas the Tank Engine* book.

I smile, I used to love *Thomas* myself, and sit down across from him with *Stormbreaker*. I've read it six times but it's the only Alex Rider they've got.

The boy stares at me, the way that little kids do. He has yellow curly hair that straggles down over his forehead, and huge brown eyes. He looks about four or five. "It's boring here," he announces as if he knows me. "There's nothing to do."

"You can read," I say, pointing at his book.

He scowls, and puts *Thomas* down. "Reading's *boring*." He folds his arms and starts rocking, crossly, in his seat. I wonder about the paper and crayons, but I guess he's the sort of kid who doesn't have the patience for drawing.

I put down my book too. I realise I'll not be reading today. "What do you like doing?"

His eyes brighten. "Soldiers. And hide and seek."

I lean back in my own seat, and rock back and forth, mimicking him. "All right," I say. "Let's play hide and seek."

He stops rocking, and giggles. "That's *silly*. There's nowhere to hide."

I look around, then point at the back wall. There is a door with a bar across it with the words FIRE EXIT on it. "Out there," I say.

"Outside?" his face falls again. "I'm not *allowed* out on my own."

I nod, "It's all right. I'll be there. So, you're not on your own."

He considers this. He looks down in the direction of the librarian and back towards the door. Then he giggles again. "All *right*," he says. "All *right*." He jumps up. He is happy now; excited. You *can* have fun in a library!

We walk to the door and I push down the metal bar. Unlike the main door it opens without a squeak. Outside is a lane, deserted except for a stray cat, scrabbling in the dirt, two green bins, and a parked white van.

I look around. "Come on," I say. I take him by the hand.

We step out and I close the door, gently, behind us. The day will heat up later; but now, outside the warmth of the library, there's an early morning chill.

"Where will I hide?" he says. He shivers and rubs his arms.

"Wait," I say.

I walk to the van, and tug the back door. It's not locked and I open it wide. Inside it's empty, save for an upside-down packing crate.

"Come on," I say, and I step in.

He follows me in, and sits immediately on the crate; holding himself straight, with his hands on his knees, like he's paying attention at school. I sit on the floor in front of him.

The van smells clean. Too clean. It makes my eyes and nose sting.

112

He looks around curiously. I don't. I don't want to look around this van. Not at him either. Not at his SpongeBob t-shirt, or his curly yellow hair, or his big brown eyes.

Finally, he chuckles. "I wonder if Daddy knows I'm gone yet."

His dad is the librarian, I realise.

"I'll go check," I say. "Quiet as a mouse now." I put my fingers to my lips.

I stand up and get out of the van again. He puts his own finger to his lips, and giggles again. Then I close the door, softly, behind me, walk to the passenger side of the van and climb in.

My dad grunts as he starts the engine.

"There's a poster up," I say, and we drive off.

Your Life in their Hands
by Tom Gordon

Scottish Arts Club Member's Award Winner 2017

The speed-camera after the Bankton Junction was covered with an orange tarpaulin which announced in black lettering 'Not In Use'.

'Just as well,' Geoffrey Bannister thought as he glanced at the speedo of his BMW and saw he was touching 95.

The dual-carriageway was quiet at three in the morning. Although the sky was clear and the moon full, there was no frost. 'A warm front coming in from the South Atlantic', the late-night weather-girl had informed him. The read-out on the dashboard told him it was 4°. 'Not bad for late February,' Geoffrey mused. 'And no more cameras till I hit the city.'

He'd only slowed at the camera at Gladsmuir since he'd left Haddington. He knew that one was still active, so he dutifully dropped to 70 – just in case. But then it was foot-down all the way. Ahead of him he could see the outline of Arthur's Seat and beyond that the expanse of The Pentland Hills, silhouetted against the pale sky that enveloped the city. It was a familiar enough vista, as the A1 into Edinburgh from its east side was Geoffrey's regular commute.

He turned off the A1 onto the city bypass and headed for the Sheriffhall roundabout. The lights changed as he approached, so he didn't have to slow down much as he swung the BMW right then left into the outskirts of the city, past the Park-&-Ride and the SQA offices, and the lights at Danderhall and The Wisp, and stopped for the first time at a red light at Ferniehill. The Edinburgh Royal Infirmary was only minutes away. As he pulled away from the lights, he pondered what awaited him.

Phoned in the middle of the night. "Stabbing," he'd been told. "Multiple wounds, male, middle-aged." He'd get the whole story soon enough.

As he turned into the white expanse of the huge hospital on the city's south side, located his designated parking place, clicked the BMW's central locking, and headed off at the trot to his regular entrance, he wondered what he would find. A patient on a trolley was the given. But the team? This was Geoffrey's final night of an on-call week and the first time he'd been contacted 'out of hours'. He'd no idea who else would be there.

Anaesthetists don't have to like the surgeons or junior doctors or even the theatre nursing-staff they work with. Most of them were OK, but it mattered little. They would do their job and he would do his – for as long as it was needed. A stabbing could be an all-nighter. Or the victim could die and Geoffrey could get home to his bed. But he had a job to do.

"Let's get it done," he mouthed as he headed to the theatre-suite.

Tommy Campbell was the first one he met. Tommy was 'one of the good guys' as Geoffrey had regularly reported, and a top-class surgeon.

"Evening, Geoffrey   or is it morning?"

"Bloody middle-of-the-night, smart-arse," Geoffrey responded. "What've we got?"

The two men were donning their scrubs and heading for the wash-basins.

"Stabbing victim," the surgeon reported. "Missed the heart but buggered up his gut. Spleen too. Right mess. We'll see what he's like when we open him up. He's on his way up from A&E."

"Drunken brawl?" Geoffrey enquired, little concerned about the man's social circumstances and more interested in his state of inebriation. Anaesthetics was tricky enough without the poor sod being pissed as well.

"No, I don't think so," Tommy responded. "Looks like he was attacked."

"Mugging? Interesting … drug take-down?"

"My God! You're a one for questions at three in the morning!"

"Keeps the brain active. Sorry!"

"Well, doesn't look like it. Just out of Saughton, they said. A revenge thing or something of the sort."

"Do we have a name?"

"Cato, I think."

Geoffrey froze. A shiver started on the back of his neck and shuddered down over his shoulders. "Cato," he mouthed. The word was no more than a whisper. Tommy Campbell had gone, so there was no chance of a response. But Geoffrey needed none. "Cato? No, it couldn't be ..."

"What couldn't be?" a voice beside him asked. Geoffrey turned to the junior doctor who'd joined him at the sinks.

"Oh, sorry, nothing, nothing at all. Just mumbling."

"No worries. I'm Chuka. Assisting tonight – or is it morning? Better get on. That's them wheeling him in now."

Things moved at speed after that.

By the time the patient was on the theatre-table, the room was buzzing. Adrenalin chased away any vestiges of tiredness and kept everyone on their mettle. But this time the buzz had a different edge to it.

"Cato?" someone said. "I know that name. Been in the news recently?"

"Yeah," came a response. "Wasn't he the guy that was done for a series of rapes down East Lothian way?"

"'Just out on parole, so the *Evening News* said."

"Did six years, didn't he?"

"Half what he was supposed to."

"Far too short."

"Someone jump him?"

"Revenge, like?"

"Aye, you can understand that."

"Maybe better if he'd croaked it."

"Could be arranged ...'Your life in their hands', eh?" Tommy Campbell had taken charge and his black humour, as well as eliciting a typical burst of laughter, served as a call to concentrate.

Geoffrey didn't laugh, though. He wasn't sure he was concentrating much either. All he could think of was that this Cato, this man he was anaesthetising so that the best surgical team in Edinburgh could repair his spilled guts, this bastard had raped his niece.

No one in the team knew that. If they did, no one had said. His niece's married name was different from his anyway. The trial had been six years ago, and Geoffrey had worked in the Borders General then. But he knew. And more than that, he was aware that his niece's husband, Martin, knew Cato was out of Saughton too.

Geoffrey and Martin had met up for a drink the previous week, when the story had broken in the *Evening News*. It had raked up some painful stuff.

"Fucking bastard," Martin had said.

"Only six lousy years," Geoffrey had agreed.

The two men had nursed their wrath over a couple of hours of drinking. It was unspeakably hellish. By the time they were sharing a taxi home, the effect of several pints had served to fuel Martin's anger further. Geoffrey had done little to calm him down.

"The fucker," was the last thing Martin had mouthed as the taxi dropped Geoffrey off. "He doesn't deserve his freedom, or his life. Maybe I'll do him myself one day."

And here was Cato now. 'Your life in their hands'. He could hear the surgeon's words. 'Your life in our hands ...' was all Geoffrey could think about. Your life in Tommy Campbell's hands ... In Chuka's hands ... In my hands ... A botched operation; a failed procedure; too much blood-loss. "Nothing more we could do"? No one would have questioned. No investigation. No problem.

"This fucking life in our hands? O God, if there's any justice, let him die ..."

And in Martin's hands? For a second time that night, a shiver ran down Geoffrey's spine.

It was after six when they called it a day.

"Good job, team," Tommy Campbell announced as Cato was being wheeled into ITU. "Anyone fancy a bacon roll in the caff?" Chuka enquired.

There were several takers. Geoffrey wasn't one of them. He just wanted to get home.

He kept to the speed-limit all the way. Doing a ton on the A1 at three in the morning was one thing. Speeding in commuter traffic just after seven was quite another. 'Your life in their hands'.

He was passing the Tranent slip-road when his mobile rang. "What the hell? At this time of the morning?" he cursed. He flicked the Bluetooth button on the steering wheel. "Yes?" he responded gruffly.

"Hi, Geoff. Tommy Campbell here. Just wanted to tell you we lost our stabbing. Died in ITU fifteen minutes ago. Thought you'd like to know."

"Thanks," Geoffrey muttered.

"Cheers then. Hope the rest of your day goes well."

Geoffrey's eyes filled with tears. Unable to see to drive, he pulled in suddenly to the parking area just before Bankton and switched off the BMW's engine. He stayed there for a long time.

He was shaken out of his reverie by his mobile ringing again. With Bluetooth no longer active, he held the phone to his ear.

"Doctor Bannister?"

"Yes?"

"Doctor Geoffrey Bannister?"

"Yes. Who is this?"

"Lothian and Borders Police here, sir. DI Morgan. We're looking for your nephew, Martin Inglis. We've been at his house early doors, but there's no sign. Any idea where he might be?"

For the third time that night, Geoffrey Bannister started to shiver.

Trophy
by Mara Buck

Winner, Scottish Arts Club Short Story Competition 2018

The boy and his father are hunting. Sun filters through the hemlocks and warms the dry oak leaves that litter the forest floor. Acorns nestle in the leaves and frequent piles of fresh whitetail dung prove that deer are plentiful in this place that runs along behind the old graveyard. The tall man bends down and fingers a few of the hard dark pellets.

"Not cold yet. Can't be much more'n a hundred yards ahead. Best we split up here. You stick with this trail. I'll circle left."

"Big one, huh, Dad."

"Git a good clean shot and you'll have you some nice trophy. Ten-pointer for sure. But if he is, he's some smart, so don't go messing with 'im. Old ones like that been known to turn on yuh."

The boy nods silently as is his way and he watches his father disappear to the left and he checks his rifle. There is no breeze to reveal his scent. The dull crunch of the leaves under his boots is muffled by the racket of crows in the neighbouring field, the squabbling of jays in the late berries, and a thousand other noises of the woods. The autumn forest is a breathing, ever-changing entity, protecting, nurturing, and suddenly betraying those it loves best. This the boy knows and is wary.

For as long as he can remember his father has killed deer in these Maine woods and in the fields surrounding the woods, sometimes legally during season, most often not. In one of the boy's first memories, he stares out the windshield of the pickup at the midnight images of a doe and her fawn stunned by the headlights, the doe's ballerina legs crumpling as his uncle drills her from the passenger window, tossing her quivering body into the rear, his father gunning the engine onto the highway from the field where they had been waiting in ambush, the fawn raising its head in surprise, still stunned by the light and the noise and the scent of blood, its eyes huge in the reflected taillights. The boy twists around between the two men and watches the fawn recede and witnesses the doe's death agony in the pickup bed. When she is at last silent, the boy turns back to face the windshield and says nothing.

The old chest freezer in the rear shed is perpetually crammed with venison. Smaller packets of foil-wrapped rabbit and squirrel and partridge stuff the corners, but the great bulk of the artfully-arranged hoard is meat from this buck and that doe. Skins dry along the pine-lath walls and hooves and antlers hang from the rafters. "Gonna make me a good livin' someday makin' hat racks outta all this. Yessuh. Body could do some fine with that."

But his father never quite gets around to it, so throughout the years the parts multiply and form intricate shadows in the dusty light from the one small window. Whenever the freezer lid is opened and the neon bulb snaps on, the room springs alive with hooves and antlers and the smell of blood is strong although the meat is glacial. If his mother calls for a roast to defrost for dinner, the boy burrows under the hay in the friendly barn or makes himself scarce in the attic. He will not venture into the back shed.

All freshly-killed deer must hang to bleed-out. Bodies are suspended within the L between the kitchen and the shed, inside to avoid thieving animals and the nosy eyes of the law. Tongues loll from dead mouths and dark eyes cloud and legs stiffen and the deer become different things entirely. Things without life. Stolen things.

"Just meat on the hoof, all it is. Same's steak. Ain't nobody gonna tell me what I can and can't kill. Put here for food, plain and simple. Easy eatin' and mighty good too. Ain't nobody gonna stop me from takin' what I want."

The boy has heard his father and his uncle rant all his life about the rules and regulations of hunting. He remains wise and keeps his own counsel, avoiding a stinging slap and a hungry bedtime. He himself dodges most of the blows, but at night in his attic room he hears the thwack-thwack-thwack of angry fists, regular as gunfire echoing up the stairs and he covers his head with the welcoming quilt and stuffs his pillow into his mouth until sleep comes. In dreams he often visits that bewildered fawn standing alone in the field and sometimes he morphs into the fawn with the horror deep inside that his mother is dead and will soon be eaten. He dreams of hides and antlers and hooves and clear dark eyes that glaze with blood. His mother has dark eyes, bruised with blue and longing. From these dreams the boy wakes in silent terror and stares blankly until dawn.

In the puckerbrush running next to the abandoned cemetery, close to this very spot, the previous year his uncle drops a huge buck with a single shot.

"Trophy, boy. Yessuh. One friggin' rack." His father hoots and hollers and rushes over, but the boy remembers the tangle of surplus antlers in the back shed and says nothing, stepping aside, turning away as far as possible from the smell of death. The two men loop a rope around the still-twitching feet, hobbling them together, toss another noose around the arched neck, truss the buck to drag it headfirst to preserve those antlers. The men swear and struggle with two-hundred pounds of uncooperative weight as the carcass catches on junipers and snags on young birch at the edge of the woods. The boy lugs all three rifles, cartridge belts slung over his shoulders like a third-world revolutionary. He keeps his head low and thinks his own thoughts.

The brothers grunt and strain but, once they reach the old graveyard, the going gets far easier. It is only a short drag ahead to the pickup parked in the field beyond.

The boy reaches the far side first, gently places the guns on the grass, perches on the crumbling stonewall, watches a pair of squirrels. Behind him from the graveyard comes the strangest sound, like a whoosh of air released from a tyre. He hears a scream and his father yells, "Jesus. Oh, sweet Jesus. Bro! No, oh no!"

The boy runs to the scream and sees his uncle has tripped over a fallen tombstone and tumbled backward where his own weight has impaled him on the sharp points of the buck's antlers, driving them through his lungs until they form a surreal coat-rack poking through the front of his vest. The buck's head cradles him like a lover as he dies, joined now as a part of the animal. A delicate snow has coated the ground the night before and the boy notices that the blood of the man and the blood of the buck decorate that white with exactly the same colour red and he feels such sorrow for them both.

On this day in the woods, the year of his own trophy yet-to-be, his mind turns over these memories like a tongue prodding the vacancy of a lost tooth, thoughtfully, speculatively, leading to no conclusion but the certainty of the loss. The boy knows this forest, is intimate with its sounds and smells and though he has yet to meet a girl to love, he feels she should be like the forest, strong and secretive and ever-changing. He in his liminal mind vows to protect that love from violence, from theft, from rape, from those who would do harm to the truth of that which he holds closest. The forest throbs, a heartbeat to match his own, and he is peaceful waiting there for something to appear.

He hears measured footfalls in the dry leaves and he looks toward the visible sky at the edge of the woods where the graveyard begins. Through the screen of the lower branches he sees the silhouette of that enormous buck, stepping precisely, head erect, antlers like a noble crown. The deer looks directly at him and acknowledges his presence but is not afraid of him, the man-child in the brush, an innocent fawn of no consequence. A more muffled crunch, a flattened tread approaches to one side of the buck and the boy glimpses his father creeping closer, getting into sure-fire range, bearing down on his prey. They are both within the boy's sightline now, the man and the deer, and the buck continues to stare at him and inclines his royal head ever so slightly.

He feels the forest pulse about him, remembers all that has gone before and yet he is a boy, and though he does love his father, the tall man he yearns to please, he is now the fawn caught in the headlights, innocence terrified by violence, and he aims and squeezes the trigger as he has been taught.

Murdo's Journey
by Mary Fitzpatrick

Scottish Arts Club Short Story Commendation 2018
Winner, Isobel Lodge Award 2018

From the age of fifteen Murdo McLeod knew his fate; three days after leaving school he was standing in Mr Munroe's shop, wrapped in an oversized apron, doling out loose tea and rashers of bacon. Murdo didn't really mind; it wasn't as if he wanted to be a teacher or a doctor or a pearl diver, he was really quite happy, listening to gossip, counting out change, sniffing cheese and butter to make sure they weren't rancid. But that was before Aunt Flora came to stay.

***

Recently widowed Aunt Flora, wearing cerise stilettos, tightly belted white raincoat, headscarf depicting Parisian hotspots, tottered unsteadily down the ferry gangplank on toothpick legs; stepping onto the quay she swayed uncertainly and looked around her; spotting Murdo and his mother she fluttered her fingers (Murdo noticed they were tipped with cherry coloured nail polish) and swayed towards them. Murdo bent awkwardly to kiss his aunt; she offered him a cheek with a flirtatious moue; at that moment, breathing in deeply, absorbing her scent, 4711 cologne and face powder, Aqua Net hairspray and Pond's face cream, Murdo knew that things were about to change.

Soon he was drawn in by that ineffable thing Aunt Flora called *je ne sais quoi*; that, and the clothes she'd brought with her to the island. Lying back on her bed, ash from a half smoked cigarette dangling, she'd watch him through half closed eyes as he tenderly explored the wonders within her wardrobe, the midnight blue grosgrain fishtailed silk gown, the mustard yellow sateen swing coat, the rose pink linen suit, the velvet and tweed, tartan and silk; then Murdo would turn to surveying her hats – pillbox, berets, knitted pixies, pom-poms, tassels, veils, waxen cherries – before reaching up onto the top shelf to retrieve a black and white straw number the size of a cartwheel, the one she'd worn on her wedding day.

When Aunt Flora whispered conspiratorially, "You like them, don't you son?" Murdo nodded dumbly, lowering his big, knuckly head; he didn't know why but running his fingers over Aunt Flora's clothes and hats filled him with a desire he'd never before experienced, a desire which he knew could really only be fulfilled in one way.

***

Three years later, in the April Murdo turned eighteen, Aunt Flora complained of pains in her chest and throat; at Murdo's mother's suggestion she took to drinking a cordial distilled from the mayflowers; by the time she went to see Doctor Baxter her already skinny body was ravaged; come summer's end, she was gone. A week after the funeral Murdo moved into her room. When his mother questioned him about this he said, "I've always wanted this one, it's brighter than mine." Closing the door on her he looked around; now everything – the red leather photo album, the kidney shaped dressing table, the wooden jewellery box with the painted poodle on the lid, the clothes, the shoes, the hats – *everything* was his. And so, over the next few weeks, Murdo began inhabiting Aunt Flora, painting his face with her makeup, enjoying the sensation of her slim, silver bracelets jingle and settle on his arm. He longed to smooth on a pair of fine, silk stockings but was afraid to shave his legs in case he was caught in the act; he also longed to stroke *Cherries in the Snow* lacquer onto his finger nails but didn't dare, realising that the smallest fleck of paint would betray him. But every evening when he came back from the grocery store he'd put together different outfits: teaming a kilt with a red cable knit jumper, the one with pearl buttons at the shoulder, he'd become Greer Garson in *Random Harvest*; in wide legged blue woollen slacks and white silk blouse he was transformed into Katherine Hepburn. 'Perfect, perfect,' he'd whisper, even though the mirror told him that his legs were too long for the trousers, his feet too large for the dainty shoes, his fingers too thick for Aunt Flora's cocktail rings.

***

"It's time to be getting up, dear."

"I won't be going to the kirk today, Mother, I think I'm coming down with the flu." Murdo could feel his mother hesitating outside his

125

bedroom door.

"Do you want me to make you some tea?"

"No, Mother, please don't worry, I'd rather just go back to sleep."

"Well, I'll not be long, I'll heat you up some soup when I get back."

When Murdo heard the front door close he leapt out of bed; crossing to the wardrobe he pulled out one of his favourite pieces, a long black silk jersey gown with bugle beading which moved sensually on its hanger. Shrugging off his flannelette pyjamas he slipped it over his head and, as the soft material warmed his naked skin and his thin fingers caressed the beads which jittered and glinted in the flinty morning light, he relaxed into sensuous pleasure,

"Where would Aunt Flora have worn this?" he wondered. Not here, not on the island, no, it would've been in the city, at a dance in *The Locarno* maybe, or perhaps at the pictures, seeing something starring Marilyn, then on to dinner, sashaying down Buchanan Street on Uncle Frank's arm to some fancy place, "Somewhere," as she used to say with a wry puckering of her perfectly plucked eyebrows. "You eat spaghetti with a fork."

Crossing to the dressing table Murdo opened the poodle-painted make up box and took out several lipsticks, rejecting *Summer Poppy* – too harsh – and *Cashmere Pink* – too insipid. Instead he plumped for *Egyptian Sands*, a beigey coral which would be perfect for a sophisticated night of dining and dancing; and, just to finish, a fine dusting of face powder, not too much, just a dab or two across his long nose and bony brow. Jewellery? The monkey brooch and then, yes, the gold bracelet inlaid with turquoise and paste sapphires. In the mirror he didn't see a man with sea green eyes, smooth black hair and unshaven stubble, he saw someone else, someone he had long wanted to meet, the person he'd been searching for. Opening the bedroom door, he slipped downstairs, into the kitchen, where he filled the kettle and began to prepare his breakfast tray, imagining what Joan Crawford might take in the morning. Unfortunately, there was no grapefruit, nor any Californian orange juice, but they did have homemade marmalade, a wheaten loaf, even coffee, the liquid kind that came in a bottle, that

126

would just have to do, not quite up to Miss Crawford's standards, of course, but – glancing up from his preparations – he met his mother's startled eyes staring in at him through the kitchen window.

Sitting at the kitchen table, Murdo's mother rubbed at his face with a rough cloth, scrubbing away the *Egyptian Sands* and the face powder; pulling him up by the elbow she thrust him out of the kitchen door, shouting, "Get up to that bedroom and get those damnable rags off your back."

Later that afternoon Reverend Pringle was summoned to give his own forthright opinions on the situation. "I hate to say it, Mrs McLeod, but your sister was a loose woman."

"Aye, Mr Pringle, I also hate to say it but I have to agree."

Here both she and Reverend Pringle glared at Murdo, like two farmers sizing up a runtish bull calf.

"Unfortunately, Mrs McLeod, you introduced a snake into the bosom of your family. I suggest that you cleanse this house of all her filth, those clinging dresses and pots of paint with which she plastered her Jezebel face." Reverend Pringle stood and pulled his long black coat around his long snake like body. "And, Murdo, I also suggest that you take this as a lesson. Your mother and I have decided that, on this one occasion, we will turn a blind eye to this base abnormality but if it happens again …" He glanced at Mrs McLeod; when she gave a small, surreptitious nod Reverend Pringle continued. "You know, there are institutions which take unfortunates who do not fit into society and I'm sure your mother and Dr Baxter would, if necessary, take measures to ensure that you receive appropriate treatment."

***

Early next morning a tall, skinny woman tottered down the ferry gangplank onto the quayside in Oban, wearing a tightly belted white raincoat which didn't even reach her knobbly, black-silk-stockinged knees; underneath the coat she wore a fine, emerald-green and blue-striped shantung dress; on her feet, somewhat incongruously, were a pair of old white tennis shoes; finally, fluttering like a bird in the strong westerly, a large black and white straw hat perched on her dark head.

127

The woman hesitated before picking up her suitcase then, turning resolutely towards the train station, she found herself merging into the stream of pedestrians; hurrying along, ignoring the curious glances, she raised her large head and breathed in deeply, inhaling like a benign breath on the damp air just the slightest hint of *4711* cologne.

The Poppy Season
by Michael Callaghan

Scottish Arts Club Short Story Commendation 2018
Scottish Arts Club Member's Award 2018

The room was elegant but sparsely furnished. There were no pictures on the wall, no vases of flowers on the table, no books in the mahogany bookcase. The resonating *ticks* from the pendulum clock above the unlit fireplace were the only sounds disturbing the silence. Beside the fireplace was a sweeping bay window that overlooked the driveway and garden.

In the middle of the room were two chesterfield sofas. On the larger of these sat a woman and a little girl. The little girl sat back, arms folded in a self-hugging gesture, eyes fixed straight ahead. The woman sat leaning forward, hands on her knees, alert; like she was waiting for something.

Finally, the woman stood up. Tutting irritably, she walked towards the window. "It really is too bad of them," she said. She pushed back her glasses and glanced at the clock. "If they consider that security may have been compromised, Henderson should *be* here. *Now.*"

She looked outside. It was already growing dark. Across the driveway behind the lawn were the flower beds. They were full of pale pink roses and bright yellow chrysanthemums. Interspersing these were small clusters of poppies; blood-red and black and fierce. A storm had been forecast and the wind was already picking up. The woman watched the poppies swaying and flailing in the rising wind, and she shivered.

"You know, my dear, I've never liked poppies. I watched *The Wizard of Oz* when I was little and Dorothy almost died in the field of poppies – or at least almost went to sleep for *ever* – which is somehow worse. Since then they've terrified me. They grow on disturbed ground, you know. That's why they get associated with war and destruction, because of those battlegrounds. It's almost like the petals have fed on the blood in the ground beneath them. And that's what I think of them

– flowers that seem nice but, are horrible, dark things, that feed on pain and misery and death."

She looked back at the little girl. The girl continued to stare straight ahead, as if she hadn't heard anything the woman had said. The woman's expression softened. She walked back and sat down again.

"I'm sorry my dear," she laid a hand on the girl's shoulder. "I shouldn't be talking about such things. Remember, Mr Henderson will be here soon. I've heard he's a good man. When you're with him, you'll be safe. Perfectly safe."

And, as if on cue, cutting through the silence, came a distant *click* from outside, followed by a faint whirring noise. It was the sound of the security gates opening at the far end of the driveway.

The woman gasped and stood up again, "Well – at *last*. I do believe that's him." She clasped her hands together, then unclasped them.

There was the sound of a car crunching up the gravel driveway, of a car door slamming, then of footsteps approaching. Finally, the doorbell rang. It was piercing in the too-quiet room. Even though she was anticipating it, the woman started.

She looked down at the girl. "Are you ready, my dear? Well, I know you'll never be ready. But as ready as you can be?"

The girl hesitated, then nodded; slowly, but firmly.

The woman smiled. "That's my brave girl. I know this is difficult. But you'll be *safe* now. If things could be different ..." she sighed. "But your dad ... well, people make choices in life and take the consequences. Try not to hate him – to hate *us* – too much. All right?"

The girl nodded again.

The woman walked to the front door. She hesitated. "Daffodils." she called out.

The voice came back. "Sunflowers."

Those were the arranged passwords. She opened the door.

The man looked tall and solid and vaguely handsome. He had a crew cut and wore a charcoal woollen suit and a hat which partially shadowed his face. He stood at the doorway, making no attempt to enter the body of the room.

"You're late," she said. She looked pointedly at the clock above the fireplace.

The man shrugged. "Roadworks, and bad weather. Got here when I could."

She looked at him appraisingly. "You seem taller than your photograph."

He smiled. "Photographs can be misleading. You look younger than yours."

She nodded, a little uncertainly. "All right. Well, please sit down, Mr Henderson." She gestured towards the smaller of the sofas. The man looked at his watch, hesitating. But eventually he sat where she had indicated. She sat opposite him, back beside the girl.

"Is Mr ...?" he began.

She shook her head. "My husband is upstairs. He doesn't want to be here for this," she paused, as if mulling something over in her mind, glanced at the girl, then turned back to him. "I need you to know something Mr Henderson. My daughter knows what is happening, but, not surprisingly, she is having some difficulty ... digesting everything. I have explained what my husband has done. In return for helping the police, for being a witness at this trial, he will be ...well rewarded. But there are people out there ready to do bad things to us. To stop him testifying. And so we have to live somewhere else. And with that rumour today, that security has been compromised, the decision has been taken that we must now all separate. So, for a while, we can't be together. Not at first. Not for a few months at least. But one day ..."

She leaned over and kissed the little girl's head. "One day we'll all be together again."

The man nodded. "All right," he said. He stood up. "I did want to speak to ..." He hesitated, "But I don't suppose it matters. As long as I have the little girl." He looked, for the first time, at the girl. "Come on sweetheart. You're safe with me." He held out his hand.

At first the girl didn't move. Then she got up and, haltingly, walked towards him. Just before she reached him, she turned back towards the woman, and opened her mouth, like she was going to say something. And the woman ran forward and with what sounded like a sob, enveloped her arms around the girl, grasping her so tight that it looked that she could hardly breathe.

Finally, she stood up. "Goodbye, my darling." She gave a half smile, and rubbed her eyes with her fingers. Her voice seemed to crack slightly. "You're safe now. Remember that. Remember everything I said."

***

He kept his eyes on her as he drove, observing her from his windscreen mirror. He thought how small, how vulnerable she looked; that white skin almost bluish below those huge eyes; that tiny face lost under that mass of brown curls.

These jobs didn't get any easier, he thought. The thought made him oddly sad. She wasn't saying anything. Silence all the way. Well, that wasn't unusual. And he was okay with that. He wasn't a talker himself. Still, maybe he should say something.

"It's a great thing your dad's doing. Thanks to him, a bad man – a *very* bad man – will go to prison for a long time. He's a hero. You should be very proud of him."

No answer. Her face was turned to look out of her side window. He looked at her still, pale face; at her big, unblinking eyes. It was like she was catatonic, he thought.

His eyes turned back to the road.

"Has it been five minutes?"

He almost jumped in his seat. He checked his mirror again. The girl was looking at him now, through the mirror. Boy, it was almost creepy how those big eyes were staring at him like that.

He recovered himself.

"Five minutes for what, sweetheart?"

"Since we left. Has it been five minutes?"

He glanced at the dashboard clock. *What was this about?*

"About five minutes, yeah. Why?"

"She said that was how long I had to wait."

"She?" he was confused. "Who?"

"That lady. The one who killed Mummy and Daddy. She arrived a little while before you did. She made us go upstairs and pointed the gun at them and … Mummy said … please, no, don't … But she did anyway. She told me she was sorry but Daddy was going to make a friend of hers very sad and he had to be stopped. She told me she wouldn't kill me as long as I promised to wait five minutes and then tell you what had happened, and what would happen to anyone else who made her friend sad. So I promised."

The girl turned and looked out of her window as the car brakes screeched. All along the grass verge at the side of the road, she could see reams of poppies. The poppies were writhing in the rain and the wind and the fading light. Swathes of red and black, waving and beckoning to her.

"It's all right. It's been five minutes," she said

A Story the Span of Your Brow
by Kirsti Wishart

Scottish Arts Club Short Story Finalist 2018

A hat shop might not have seemed the most obvious place for a writer's residency, yet after a trying time for Gail, it proved the perfect fit. A terrible newspaper review of her last novel caused her not only to sink into the writing doldrums but also to start avoiding one of her favourite shops. She'd often paused outside the windows of The Milliner's Tale, struck by the beauty and craftsmanship of the crowning glories on display although, curiously, had never stepped inside. She felt her head too small to deserve such attention, the childhood taunts of *Pea-head* whenever she dared to wear a bobble-hat leading her to feel she'd be a fraud if she went in to browse with no intention of buying. That self-consciousness coupled with the by-line photo of Jack McCain, the extravagantly moustachioed reviewer who'd blasted her 'lazy characterisation' and 'reliance on coincidence', showing him slyly tipping the brim of his fedora, caused her to walk briskly past one of her formerly favourite pauses in her strolls about the city.

One afternoon however, a fierce blast of hailstones in April led her to take shelter in the shop's doorway, an icy shift in wind-direction forcing her inside. The shower quickly passed yet Gail remained, gazing in wonder at the artistry that had gone into each elegant design, marvelling at the colour choices, the soft pinks and lilacs, the peacock flourishes of purple and emerald, the cosy autumnal tweeds of the snug-looking caps. For the first time since her confidence had been wrecked by bloody McCain, she felt stories stirring, her own creativity responding to the obvious pleasure in making new things each hat exuberantly represented.

Perhaps it was because she felt the need to give some reason for lingering that, in an unusual bout of forwardness, she went up to the counter assistant, a woman in her late fifties with artistic grey hair and interesting glasses. Coughing nervously, she asked, "Ever thought of having a writer on site?"

"No," came the delighted response. "Not until this very moment, what a fantastic idea! And as you're the only applicant, you're hired!"

Following a brief moment of panic, the charming enthusiasm with which her proposition was greeted along with a celebratory cup of tea caused Gail to decide fate had provided an opportunity too intriguing to run away from. That, and the half hour she'd spent there, had already proved far more stimulating than the slump of despair she'd immediately fall into on switching on her laptop. Once she'd given Elena, the assistant, who it emerged was also the owner and chief milliner, a run-down of her writing credentials, she was granted free rein to wander and observe for as long as she liked with her notebook.

In the days that followed, what impressed her most was how the skills of Elena and Heather, the co-owner, would transform each of the long-necked, blank faced mannequins on shelves lining the walls into an individual character, giving them a distinct personality. With the addition of a feather or brooch or a contrasting band of satin they could become dynamic and daring or cute and coy. Gail became fascinated by fascinators, how delicate, scarcely-there arrangements of lace and wire and downy feathers enhanced a lady's hair to a point of sophistication that would lend any wedding, garden party or race-course an extra twist of style and grace.

Sitting in a battered armchair placed in the corner of the shop, tales spun from Gail's pen. Back at home, opening her laptop became a source of excitement rather than dread as she transferred her writing onto the shop's website. There, next to photos of Heather or Elena's latest creations, appeared descriptions of the character evoked by a particular hat. A fake-fur Russian ear-warming specimen inspired the tale of Yuri, the former cosmonaut exiled in Greenwich who would walk the banks of the Thames to stave off homesickness. An explosion of pink and sparkles was the treat Rosetta, a young ballerina yet to rise from the chorus, had set her heart on once she'd been given the role of Swan Lake's Odette. A scarlet pill-box was the choice of Miss Spark, a former head-mistress and rumoured poisoner, who had nicked off an opponent's earlobe during an amateur fencing competition.

Gail revelled in discovering the power of hats, how buyers

appreciated putting them on as marking them out from the crowd and so treated them with a respect you rarely saw applied to other items of clothing. They carried away their boxed purchases with a level of care she'd only previously seen applied by those transporting cat carriers. She realised and understood their transformative effects, how computer geeks became urban dandy highwaymen when they pulled on a tricorn, how a cloche turned a Thora Hird into a Greta Garbo, a sweeping brim causing a timid second year fashion student to straighten her shoulders to match the gaze of her reflection, like a sharp-eyed Edith Head. Gail grew both to love and be wary of bunnets, the way they made any man who flopped one on with a cheeky wink about 500 times more attractive than when they'd been bare-headed.

It was perhaps wanting to tap into that magic that caused her to do what she did. Otherwise, she couldn't be sure why she didn't tell anyone she'd taken to printing out sentences she'd then cut into strips and slip under a hatband or other decorative piece, to be worn unseen. She was sure neither Elena or Heather would have minded, indeed would probably have enjoyed the mischief-making element. But it felt like over-stepping a mark, encroaching on their territory. That and Gail knew the real reason she kept quiet was she enjoyed sharing a secret between herself and the hat alone.

She regarded what she had written as instructions for use, a means of influencing the wearer. "Today I will attempt an affair with the next attractive soul I meet' for a bowler; the sunshine yellow of a wide-brimmed summer hat carrying 'When the day is as bright as I am, we will fly a kite from the top of our tenement' and 'I will tell a dark secret from my childhood to a stranger' hidden behind rosebuds decorating a jaunty half-hat.

When stories started coming back about the acts of some of the recent buyers of The Milliner's wares, Gail laughed at the thought she could possibly have been the cause. She suspected the owners, or one of the other members of staff, had caught wind of what she was up to, and unpicked a sentence from its hiding place to turn it into a publicity stunt. Their surprise when customers came back to marvel at what they'd been up to, jokily accusing their newly acquired headgear, suggested otherwise. After the respected novelist, renowned for his

136

gentle tales of city life, told them with gruesome relish he'd decided to write the true history of Burke and Hare, describing how the editions would match the notebook bound in Burke's skin, or she heard how a librarian had organised a flash-mob of madrigal singers in the reference section though, Gail felt a shiver of recognition then a thrill, as if hailstones had scoured her unprotected neck.

To her credit, when the bell of the shop tinged and Jack McCain himself appeared, announcing his arrival by lifting his fedora and asking "Ladies! What do you have to keep this glorious brain of mine warm?" Gail felt sick rather than gleeful. She bowed her head over her notebook, deciding it would be too cruel to attempt what she'd planned should this moment ever arise as he worked his way through every gentleman's hat available, a number to match the names he dropped. Finally, he settled on a fedora near identical to the one he'd come in with. Yes, it would be ridiculous to attempt any kind of voodoo. He'd only been doing his job after all.

She looked up when he asked her. "Gail, isn't it? Gail – ah ..."

"Turner. I'm – um – writer in residence here."

He gave a short laugh. "Well, yes. After reading your novel, shop-work probably is for the best. Should grant a much-needed depth of experience."

With that Gail rose, took his choice from him and carried it to the counter. "Thank you, Mr McCain. I can honestly say, after your review you gave me my opportunity here, an experience I didn't even realise I longed for."

He smirked an 'Aren't I a genius?' smile as she hid the slip of paper that read, "I will lay the head I hold across the tracks and escape in the breeze that follows."

And when, a few days later, Heather gasped and shared the news that appeared on her phone telling of the loss of a valued customer, had Gail had been wearing a hat, she'd have tossed it high.

Eleionomae, The River Nymph
by Emily Learmont

Scottish Arts Club Short Story Finalist 2018

At the age of sixty-four, Sir Alfred Leighton-Jones considered that he had achieved the pinnacle of his career. His election as a Royal Academician had resulted in the patronage of Queen Victoria, a knighthood and an exhibition of his paintings and sculptures at the new gallery of British art at Millbank. As he reclined on a chaise longue in the Peacock Hall of his mansion in Holland Park, he regarded his prized black-and-gold lacquered Japanese screen and his collection of Persian lustreware vases with a sense of deep satisfaction.

There was one aspect of his life, however, that he found to be lacking. In all these years, not one of his female admirers – and there had been many – had agreed to enter with him into the matrimonial state that seemed to be so essential to modern society.

Sir Alfred rose and strode across the hall, his dressing gown fluttering.

He paused in front of his masterpiece *Eleionomae, The River Nymph,* the painting with which he had established his reputation, a gold-medallist at the Paris Salon. He scrutinized it intently. He had rendered the nymph life-sized and nude, pale-skinned and smooth, against a background of brushwork that was intended to evoke a riverbank and bulrushes. Her dark hair was highlighted with droplets of water and in her right hand was a water lily. Sir Alfred recalled the youthful passion with which he had executed the painting. Striving by daylight and lamp-light in that grimy studio in Tottenham Court, impelled by the necessity to prove his talent, to fulfil his ambition – or else be forced to return to his job as a corset-maker in his father's shop in Charing Cross Road.

It occurred to him then that it was *Eleionomae* who was the love of his life. His obsession with her had preoccupied him for over forty years as he recreated her beauty in a series of celebrated paintings.

He got down on bended knee.

"Eleionomae, my dear. Would you do me the honour of becoming my wife?"

The surface of the painting rippled. Sir Alfred reached up and took the nymph by her hand as she stepped out of the frame. He took off his onyx signet ring and slipped it onto her finger. Then he swept her into the folds of his dressing gown and carried her up to his bedroom, rivulets of river-water, duckweed and sticklebacks cascading down the staircase.

Sir Alfred's wedding night with Eleionomae went beyond his wildest expectations, passing in a miasma of sensations that were hitherto unknown to him. There were moments of ecstasy that were as brilliant as blazes of phosphorescence, and moments when he thought that he would drown as he dived down to her watery depths. He was in awe of the perfection of her form: her slender white limbs that coiled around him; her cold moist flesh that slithered against his old dry skin. He caressed her waving tresses and sipped kisses from her lips. Yet (as he later admitted) he was always vaguely aware of her slightly marshy breath.

When Sir Alfred awoke next morning, he was surprised to find that Eleionomae was gone, leaving merely a puddle in the crumpled sheets in which two tadpoles swam.

He hurried downstairs. The nymph was in the painting again, the water lily back in her hand. However, Sir Alfred was relieved to observe that she was still wearing his ring.

"My dear?" proffered Sir Alfred. "What would you say to a jaunt up to town? We could visit the Royal Academy Summer Exhibition and take luncheon at the Cafe Royal?"

Eleionomae smiled and slid out of the frame.

"But my dear!" remarked Sir Alfred. "You can't go like that!"

He went to his studio and fetched a gown, a bonnet and a pair of boots that had been lent to him by Lady Ashby for the purpose of finishing her portrait. He dried the nymph and dressed her, pulling tight the laces of Lady Ashby's whale-bone corset.

"Delightful!" commented Sir Alfred, appraising her stylish appearance.

Next, he raced upstairs to put on a suit and wax his moustache. When he returned, he found that Eleionomae was sitting stiffly on the chaise longue, oozing miry liquid. He took her gently by the hand, picked up his ivory-topped cane from the umbrella stand and opened the front door.

"Cab!" he called, marching down the street, the nymph trailing after him.

***

Eleionomae's introduction to London society was not the triumph that Sir Alfred had so desired. In the over-crowded galleries of the Royal Academy, the marshy smell that he had previously detected grew considerably stronger. Moreover, Eleionomae left a trail of scummy slime wherever she went in which other visitors skidded.

"My dear," whispered Sir Alfred. "You appear to be dripping."

And Sir Alfred had to confess that Eleionomae was not particularly good company. She did not seem to be interested in the exhibits (the paintings with their gilded frames or the bronze and marble sculptures) and when she did express an opinion, it was in ancient Greek. He began to notice that the admirers who usually thronged around him, attracted by his fame, were backing away.

"Ruskin! My dear fellow!" Sir Alfred hailed the distinguished art critic who was dressed in his customary blue cravat. "May I introduce my wife?"

"Χαῖρε," murmured Eleionomae.

Ruskin took Eleionomae's hand and raised it to his lips – but he looked askance when a frog hopped out of her sleeve.

"Charmed …" he remarked as he drifted off.

It was then that Sir Alfred realised that Eleionomae had been surreptitiously shedding her clothes. Her gloves and bonnet were gone, her feet were bare and – to his mortification – she was attempting to loosen her bodice.

Sir Alfred put his arm around her protectively yet sorrowfully.

"Let us go home," he said.

***

On their return to the Peacock Hall, Eleionomae immediately climbed back into the painting and submerged herself up to her chin in the river. Her eyelashes seemed to Sir Alfred to be even damper than usual.

Sir Alfred withdrew to his studio where he sat for some time contemplating the canvas on his easel, without actually seeing anything. Next, he went to a stack of portfolios, selected one and took out a sheaf of paper: the preparatory drawings for *Eleionomae, the River Nymph*. He recalled making them; the model, an out-of-work milliner from Bethnal Green, posing for hours each day, standing knee-deep in a washtub full of water. He had lit fires with his unsuccessful drawings and brewed beef tea to warm her up. She was a chirpy young thing, always singing, always laughing. He wondered what had happened to her. He had heard a rumour that she had drowned herself under Blackfriars Bridge (found straggle-legged and bloated) for the sake of unrequited love

Sir Alfred sat for a while longer. Then he fetched his brushes, some tubes of paint and his palette, and took these to the Peacock Hall. He was pleased to see that Eleionomae had resumed her habitual pose, water lily in hand.

He began to retouch the painting, working rapidly, referring back-and-forth to the drawings. He replaced the green tinge of her skin with a rosy pink hue and dotted it with freckles. Next, he altered the angles of her nose and mouth, and accentuated the curves of her cheeks, filling them in with dimples. Finally, he removed all of the drops of water.

He stood back to survey his work.

The surface of the painting rippled. A girl stepped out.

"Ello, Alfie!" she said, giving him a peck on the cheek.

"Ellie, my dear!" exclaimed Sir Alfred.

The girl wrapped Eleionomae's abandoned gown around her shoulders.

"That's better," she said. "I've been ever so cold."

She looked down at the ring on her finger and smiled contentedly.

"May I 'ave a mug o' beef tea?" she requested.

Game On
by Rachael Dunlop

Scottish Arts Club Short Story Finalist 2018

"Grab hold of me," Stacey called over her shoulder. "Before I fall out of this window. I can't quite get my phone into the light."

Carl looped an arm around his girlfriend's skinny waist as she raised herself onto her tiptoes and extended her arm into the slim shaft of light that fell between the apartment buildings.

"Got it. Pull me in," she said after a few minutes. Back in the room, she checked the display on her phone. "Twenty per cent charge. That'll have to do. Did you have to rent an apartment with so little natural light, Carl?"

Carl shrugged. "I'm not a millionaire. Light costs. And maybe if you hadn't used the last of your lithium playing that game ..."

Stacey's eyes narrowed. "I'm this close to getting three stars on every level. This close." She held up a finger and thumb, pinched so close together their heavily calloused pads nearly touched.

"If we miss the notification for the flash-mob because you've got no charge on your phone ..."

"The irony is not lost on me, Carl." Her phone beeped. "Here we go." She scanned the incoming message, brows pulled low. "This is it, Carl, the big one. It's on."

The plaza outside the Ministry for Energy building was already packed with protesters by the time Stacey and Carl arrived.

"Let's get up to the front," Stacey said, grabbing Carl's hand and sliding shoulder first into the crowd. "Leo said he'd meet me there."

A slice of sunlight cut through the smog-heavy sky and, almost as one, the protesters pulled out their phones and held them aloft. Carl shielded his eyes as light bounced off the photovoltaics that covered every device. It seemed to him that the light was making a bid for freedom, using its precious energy to skip and dance, skim across the

143

prismatic panels and leap back into the sky. Carl left his phone in his pocket. His was fully charged.

"Remember," Stacey said, "it's a big deal, you meeting Leo. The fewer people who know who he is, the better."

Carl nodded. "I know, I'm honoured. So you reckon today's the day?"

"Leo says he has finally got concrete evidence that the energy rationing isn't universal." Stacey stopped, turned and spoke softly into Carl's ear. "He has video showing they are still running life-support machines in the private hospitals. That you can get all the energy you need if you pay for it. He's planning a multi-platform broadcast to expose the entire corrupt system."

How ironic, Carl thought. Not so long ago, Stacey would have been an eco-warrior, campaigning for alternative energy and reducing the carbon footprint. But then the lithium and nickel supplies bottomed out and the earthquakes in the Middle East sank the oil reserves. Since the rationing came in, the kids were all protesting to get their batteries back. This guy, Leo, though, he was different. Had them all rallied behind the idea that the energy supplies hadn't run out at all, they were just being squeezed for every ounce of profit by the energy companies and the games developers. Just a conspiracy theory, the authorities said, as if no conspiracy had ever turned out to be true.

"There he is!" Stacey pushed forwards and flung her arms around a tall man. He was older than Carl had expected, and more nondescript. The perfect subversive.

Carl hung back, letting two or three people get in front of him, then pulled out his phone and activated the 'Find Me' function. Really, he should try to get a photo of Leo, but that would be too conspicuous. Taking photos wasted battery power, hardly anyone did it any more, preferring to save their energy allowance for gaming. Looking around, he could see at least half the people here, mid-protest even, were playing on their mobile devices, thumbs flicking fast over touch-screens. There's a source of energy right there they could harvest, thought Carl. All those fingers and thumbs, swiping, flicking; pulling

144

and pushing electrons between glass and skin. Energy cannot be destroyed. That's what people forgot. Never destroyed, just converted. And controlled.

Carl elbowed his way back to where he'd left Stacey. She was hanging on Leo's arm, listening to him talk, grinning like an idiot. One word from Leo, and Carl would be relegated to ex-boyfriend status, he could see that. Not that he cared.

His phone vibrated softly in his hand. He read the message and nodded, looking around. He knew they could see him; they saw everything. The instructions were simple enough.

"Hey, Leo, care to get your hands off my girlfriend?"

Stacey unpeeled herself, ran forward to intercept him. "Carl, it's nothing, don't make a scene. We're nearly ready ..."

Carl pushed past her and, just as he had been instructed, put his right hand on Leo's shoulder. Leaning in close, he whispered in Leo's ear, "Game's up, buddy."

Carl melted back into the crowd. He could hear Stacey calling him but he kept walking, didn't look back. He didn't need to. He knew the routine. The agents would have closed in on Leo now that Carl had identified him, and unobtrusively removed him from the crowd. He hoped they left Stacey out of it – she was dumb but harmless.

He found a quiet alley then patted himself down. There it was, a small key wrapped in a twist of recycled paper stuffed into the back pocket of his jeans. They were good; he hadn't even felt them slip it in there. Oh yes, they were good. And careful; a physical key can't be hacked. His phone buzzed again. Carl smiled as he read the message. The key was for a strong box at the bank. Inside he would find a year's supply of lithium and Ni-MH batteries courtesy the energy companies. Meanwhile, the grateful games developers had credited his account with 10,000 hours of game play. His passport to freedom.

Carl flipped his phone to game mode. Really, he thought, he should wait until he got home, but ... what the hell. He slumped against the alley wall and started to play.

The Genuine Article
by Colin Armstrong

Scottish Arts Club Short Story Finalist 2018

"What are you doing here Torquil? I told you, it's not ready."

Torquil cast his eyes around the jumble of tubes and brushes in
Malcolm's studio. Discarded paint adorned every surface, including the
capacious canvas of Malcolm's t-shirt.

"I'm not here about the Rembrandt." Torquil mopped his brow with
a white linen handkerchief. The studio was oppressively close and the
smell of the oils was overpowering.

"It took me ages to find the right canvas, without any modern
chemicals in it. Something I can age convincingly. Then there's the
paint." He waved a tube menacingly at Torquil, causing him to step
back into something sticky. "The lead will probably kill me."

"Malcolm, will you stop working for a minute and listen to me?" He
picked up a rag and tried to clean his brogues. "Your life may be in
danger, but not from lead paint."

Malcolm consulted the reproduction pinned to the wall and then
applied more white paint to the ruff of the lady in black. Her husband
stared reprovingly at Torquil.

"You're such an old woman, Torquil. What on earth are you on
about?"

"Why's it so hot in here? I can hardly breathe." He ran a finger
around his yellow cravat.

"I've got a Velasquez in the oven. Ten minutes on gas mark two will
crack the surface nicely." Malcolm shook his head as Torquil flapped
his hand ineffectually in front of his face.

"All right," he said, setting down his brush and palette. "I'll put the
kettle on."

"God no! It's too hot for tea. I'll fetch us both a glass of water. Do you have any ice?"

They settled into a pair of wooden chairs in the garden. Torquil thought wryly to himself that they could do with a coat of paint. The cooling breeze was welcome, despite the tang of manure.

"Why do you live all the way out here?" Torquil surveyed the relentlessly flat farmland razed of hedgerows and trees and imagined Constable spinning in his grave.

"So that I can get on with my work without being disturbed. You bloody salesmen think it's a doddle, don't you?" He continued in a cut-glass accent in mock imitation of Torquil. "Knock me out a Rembrandt before lunch would you old fruit?" He held his glass of water with a raised little finger.

"That's not fair Malcolm. Anyway, I'm not here about the Rembrandt. We've got a problem with *Le Pigeon aux Petits Pois.*"

Malcolm blew out his cheeks and ran a speckled hand through his grey mane.

"I told you we should steer clear of Picasso. He's too easy and too expensive. It was bound to draw unwelcome attention."

"Well, it's too late now. Our Russian friend brought in Hans Richter."

"What? How could Ivan get an authority like Richter to look at a stolen painting?"

"His name's Mikhail. His henchmen grabbed Richter in Paris, bundled him into his Gulfstream and flew him to St. Petersburg. He told him to authenticate the painting or he would chop his balls off."

"Bloody hell. Not even Richter deserves that."

"Apparently Richter told him it was a fake and nothing would induce him to authenticate it."

Malcolm whistled. "Well, he's got bigger *cojones* than me. He does still have them doesn't he?"

"Oh yes, Richter cut a deal – 100,000 euros in return for the name of the forger and his silence."

"And he identified me?" Malcolm took a long pull on his water.

"Quicker than Pablo discarding a mistress."

"That bastard." Malcolm drew himself up in his chair. "No one else could have pulled it off."

"I don't want to rub it in, old boy. But you didn't pull it off, did you? And now we have a pissed-off Russian oligarch on our hands."

"Can't you just give him his money back?"

"Come on Malcolm, that won't wash. We made a fool of him. He wants revenge."

"*You* made a fool of him. I've never met the man."

"That's not the way Mikhail sees things." Torquil got out of his chair and scanned the horizon. He was pleased to see Malcolm really did live miles from anywhere.

"Wait a minute." Malcolm knitted his brows. "How do you know all this?" Torquil looked at him as fearfully as one of the damned in Bosch's Last Judgement.

"You Judas." Malcolm leapt to his feet and grabbed Torquil by his Saville Row lapels. "You've led them here haven't you?" He began shaking Torquil violently.

"Stop it Malcolm." Tears were running down Torquil's face. "Please stop. No one is coming."

Malcolm violently pushed him away. "Look at you, blubbering like a schoolgirl. It's pathetic."

"You've no idea what I've been through." Torquil dried his eyes with his handkerchief. "His thugs dragged me out of bed in the middle of the night. They put a hood over my head and plastic ties around my wrists and ankles. Then they threw me in the boot of their car and drove around for hours. When they took off the hood we were in some kind of industrial shed and I was examining the barrel of Mikhail's gun."

"Dear God." Malcolm took another drink of his water and looked at the glass in disgust. "I need something stronger." Eager to placate him, Torquil fetched him a whisky. Malcom took the brimming glass from Torquil's shaking hand and swallowed an inch of malt.

"But here you are as right as rain, eh? A wimp like you couldn't fight his way out of that situation. You've cut a deal, you worm. You've sold me down the river."

"You have to understand. I was terrified. He was going to kill both of us." Torquil sat back in his chair and looked glumly at Malcolm. "But I managed to persuade him that there was something you loved more than life itself."

Malcolm's faced dropped. "What are you talking about?"

"I told him that if you were unable to paint it would destroy you."

Malcolm drank more whisky to try and quell his nausea. "What's he going to do to me?"

"He's decided to cut off your fingers, Malcolm."

"The barbarian!" Malcolm leapt to his feet and looked around wildly, as if expecting imminent attack.

"For Heaven's sake sit down. No one is coming."

Malcolm rounded on Torquil. "What do you mean?" he shouted into his face. "How do you know?"

"No one is coming because I'm already here. You see Malcolm, that's *my* punishment. Mikhail expects me to do it. He gave me a pair of bolt-cutters. They're in the boot."

Malcolm threw back his head and roared with laughter.

"You? A preening peacock like you?" He wiped tears from his eyes. "He doesn't know you very well, does he?"

Torquil chose to ignore the insult. "Yes, well, that's why I came to see you, Malcolm. You're much cleverer that I am. I thought you might come up with a way out of this."

Malcolm took a large swig of inspiration.

"Ha!" Malcolm's exclamation made Torquil jump. "We do what we've always done, old boy. We make a fake. I'll mock up some bloody stumps and you can take some snaps as proof of the dreadful deed." He gurned hideously, as if wracked by agonising pain. Torquil sighed.

"He wants your fingers, Malcolm. The genuine article. I can't fob him off with rubber ones from a joke shop."

"How hard can fingers be to come by? We could bribe an undertaker or a doctor." He snapped his threatened digits. "Of course, one of your daughters ... what's her name? Clarissa?"

"Camilla."

"Yes, yes ... the plain one. Isn't she a doctor?" Malcom drained his glass.

"She's a GP. But I think someone might notice if her patients' fingers started to go missing."

Malcolm sat forward in his chair and put his hand to his head. "You know with all this excitement, I'm really feeling rather peculiar."

"As it happens, I did speak to Camilla."

"Good man ... good man." Malcolm sounded distracted. He was having difficulty concentrating.

"I told her I was having trouble sleeping. She prescribed some pills for me."

Malcolm slumped back in his chair and tried to focus on Torquil, but his sight was blurred.

"She said they would knock me out in no time."

"Torquil, I don't understand ..." Malcolm's eyes rolled back in his head. After a couple of minutes contemplating his prone form, Torquil rose from his chair and gave Malcolm a good shake. When he didn't stir, Torquil went out to his car.

Full Circle
by Christina Eagles

Winner, Edinburgh International Flash Fiction Award 2018

Picnic eaten, and Mum and Dad settled in deck chairs with a Thermos, our brothers would send Nuala and me to draw circles in the wet sand. This task was our responsibility, our contribution to the ritual of the beach.

Oblivious of the wide-winged gulls, ignoring the fall of waves at the sea edge, Nuala and I worked. We decorated our lines with shells and seaweed and smooth, round pebbles. Our skins were sticky with salt water.

After Nuala learned about circles at school, we laboured to make ours perfectly round. Her hair slipped loose and whipped across her cheeks as she traced out circumferences with a driftwood radius. Then she did King Arthur and told me they were sanctuaries. We strengthened their powers with incantations we called magic.

When our brothers came back from the far ends of the beach, we played tig. Our spaces were dens. We dodged and chased across the sand, nipping from one to the next. Nuala and I jumped inside, squealing. We giggled as the boys skidded to a halt outside, snarling in mock fury, unable to reach us over the boundaries we had built.

Today, Nuala talks of secondaries and treatment options. Her face is grey beneath the red headscarf that hides her naked scalp. She asks will I watch her girls. I taste salt on our cheeks. I chant our charms in my head as I place my arms about her, in a circle that I make perfectly round.

Same Skin, Different Body
by Debbie Taggio

Edinburgh International Flash Fiction Award, Commendation, 2018

My life changed forever the day I lost my daughter. Her diary lay on the bed – pages open – neat, looped handwriting inviting me into a secret world. I closed the book, side-eyeing it as I flicked the duster around the room; motherly curiosity destroying an unspoken code.

She described hating her body, averting her eyes every time she showered, avoiding the mirror – an exercise in getting through life one day at time, hoping for change one way or the other. The stupid advert about loving the skin you're in when it wasn't her skin that was the problem – it was the inside making the outside wrong.

As I let go of the past and put her clothes into bin bags, I searched within for answers. That sly drag on a cigarette before knowing I was pregnant. Did I drink too much, eat soft cheese during pregnancy, was I too busy with work, too preoccupied setting right a failing marriage? Was I to blame? I missed the little things – manicures, watching chick-flicks; I think she did them for me – a selfless act because I knew she was a tomboy, happiest in hoodie and jeans.

A final hug, I don't want to let her go and my tears soak into the surgical gown for the girl I'm losing. He says I haven't lost him, that he's always going to be my funny, quirky, idiotic child – same skin, different body. My life changed forever the day I met my son.

Daffodils with Apples
by Claire Fuller

Edinburgh International Flash Fiction Award, Commendation, 2018

The blowflies arrive, and then their offspring. No one rings the doorbell. The daffodils in their vase droop and double over, as though in pain. The apples in the fruit bowl collapse in on themselves. The rain beats on the studio skylights, and the colours on her dropped palette dull and harden. Dust settles over everything: books, cups, toothbrush, face. Months of sun cracks the paint on her canvasses and solidifies what's left in the tubes.

The post piles up on the floor under the letterbox. Circulars and two more letters from galleries, containing polite rejections. She uses no gas, nor electricity; there is no rent to pay on the studio. She doesn't have a television. Her bank account is open but empty.

No one knocks. Two crisp leaves find their way in under the studio door. A house spider weaves a funnel-shaped web under the draining board and lays an egg sac. Mice taste the badger hair on the end of her brushes, chew the handle of the palette-knife she still holds, nibble on a toe. Snow piles up on the windowsills; melts.

Under the floorboards a pipe rusts and a slow leak starts, saturating the wood. In the apartment below, a yellow stain appears on the ceiling, and the paper bubbles and then bursts. Someone knocks on her door and knocks again. Someone else breaks the door down.

Her painting of a vase of daffodils next to a bowl of apples sells for £100,000.

Madeleine from Macclesfield
by Marilyn Jeffcoat

Scottish Arts Club Member's Award for Flash Fiction

It was in the book I picked up from the train seat. A carefully folded sheet of blue notepaper and, in an educated hand, these words:

Dearest Freddie
There is No Future
I Can't Go On
Madeleine

What despair lay behind those words; the staccato style and the capital letters. I had to find Madeleine. Should I put an advert on Gumtree or in the Metro?

Then another thought struck me. A young person would have sent a text, and the notepaper was old-fashioned these days. Someone like that wouldn't look at Gumtree or read the Metro. I had boarded the train in Macclesfield. There can't be that many Madeleines in Macclesfield. Perhaps a classified ad in the local newspaper would be better. Or a radio appeal.

Who was Freddie? Perhaps it was a girl. Frederica. It was more the sort of note a woman would write to a friend. A lot left unsaid, but the meaning clear to someone close. Why did she leave the note in the book? She must have meant to post it or deliver it when she got off the train. Clearly, she had left the book behind in her distress.

A voice announced the train was terminating – I collected together my bags and, for the first time, saw the back cover of the book. It contained a list of titles by the same author:

Dearest Freddie
There is No Future
I Can't Go On
Madeleine

About the Scottish Arts Trust Story Awards

www.storyawards.org

The Scottish Artists' Club was founded in 1873 by a group of artists and sculptors, including Sir John Steell, Sculptor to Queen Victoria, and Sir George Harvey, President of the Royal Scottish Academy. For twenty years they met in a series of premises around the West End of Edinburgh. In 1894, the building at 24 Rutland Square was purchased as a meeting place for men involved in all arts disciplines and Lay Members (those not professionally engaged in the arts) were also welcomed into the Club. To reflect the widening membership, it was renamed the Scottish Arts Club.

It was not until 1982, following contentious debate, that women were admitted as club members. In 1998, Mollie Marcellino became its first female President. Until her death in 2018, Mollie was also an avid reader for the Scottish Arts Club Short Story Competition.

The idea for the competition, which is open to writers worldwide, developed out of the Scottish Arts Club Writers Group. Alexander McCall Smith has long been a supporter and honorary member of the Club, which has sometimes featured in his Scotland Street novels. He volunteered to be our chief judge and has remained in that role ever since. He is aided by a team of readers whose primary qualifications are a love of short stories and a willingness to read, debate, defend and promote their favourites through successive rounds of the competition. All stories reaching the penultimate round have been read at least 40 times by our readers and most have been subject to passionate debate.

The short story prize money increased from a first prize of £300 in 2014 to £1,000 by 2017. In that year we also launched the Isobel Lodge Award, named after a dear friend and member of the Writers Group. This £500 prize is given to the top story entered in the competition by an unpublished writer born, living or studying in Scotland.

In 2018 we introduced the Edinburgh International Flash Fiction Competition, with novelist Sandra Ireland as the chief judge. Sandra

155

won the first of our short story competitions with her story, *The Desperation Game*, which lends its title to this anthology.

We are committed to supporting and promoting the work of short story and flash fiction writers. Every finalist since the competition began has a page on our website through which they may promote their work as a writer, and share insights and photographs describing their writing practise. Take a look at The Writers pages on www.storyawards.org.

We also enjoy celebrating the work of our finalists at the annual and always sold-out story awards dinner held at the Scottish Arts Club.

The story awards are managed through the Scottish Arts Trust, a charity registered as the Scottish Arts Club Charitable Trust (charity number SC044753). All funds raised through our competitions, which also include the annual Scottish Portrait Awards, are used to promote the arts in Scotland.

Sara Cameron McBean
Director of the Scottish Arts Trust Story Awards
Edinburgh 2019